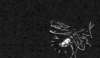

Palefire © 2015 MK Reed and Farel Dalrymple

Published by Secret Acres

Secret Acres
237 Flatbush Ave, #331
Brooklyn, NY 11217

SA028

Printed in USA.

Contributing Editor Greg Means

Library of Congress PCN: 2015930723

ISBN-13: 978-0-9888149-7-4
ISBN-10: 0988149-7-8

Mk Reed Farel Dalrymple

palefire

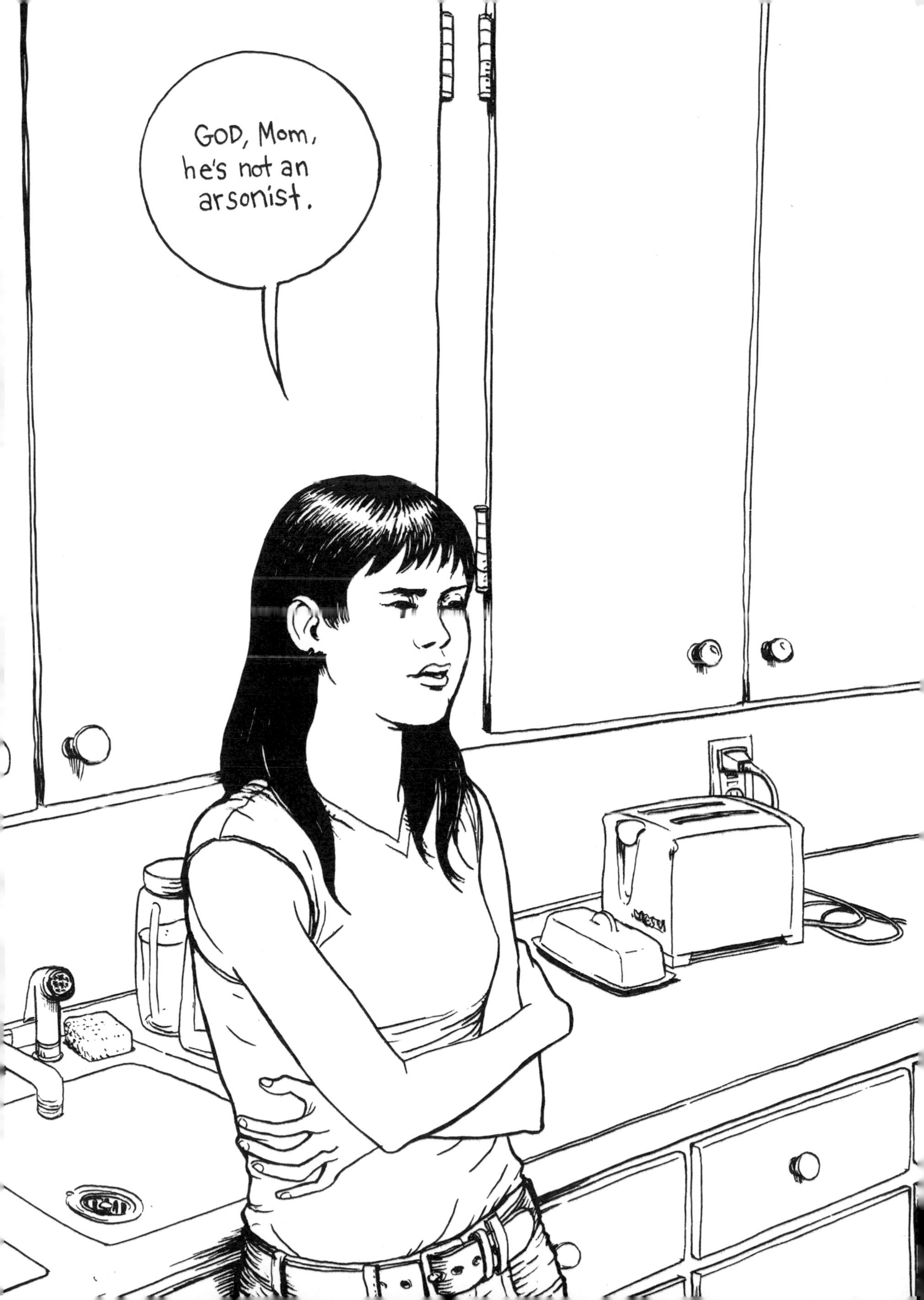
GOD, Mom, he's not an arsonist.

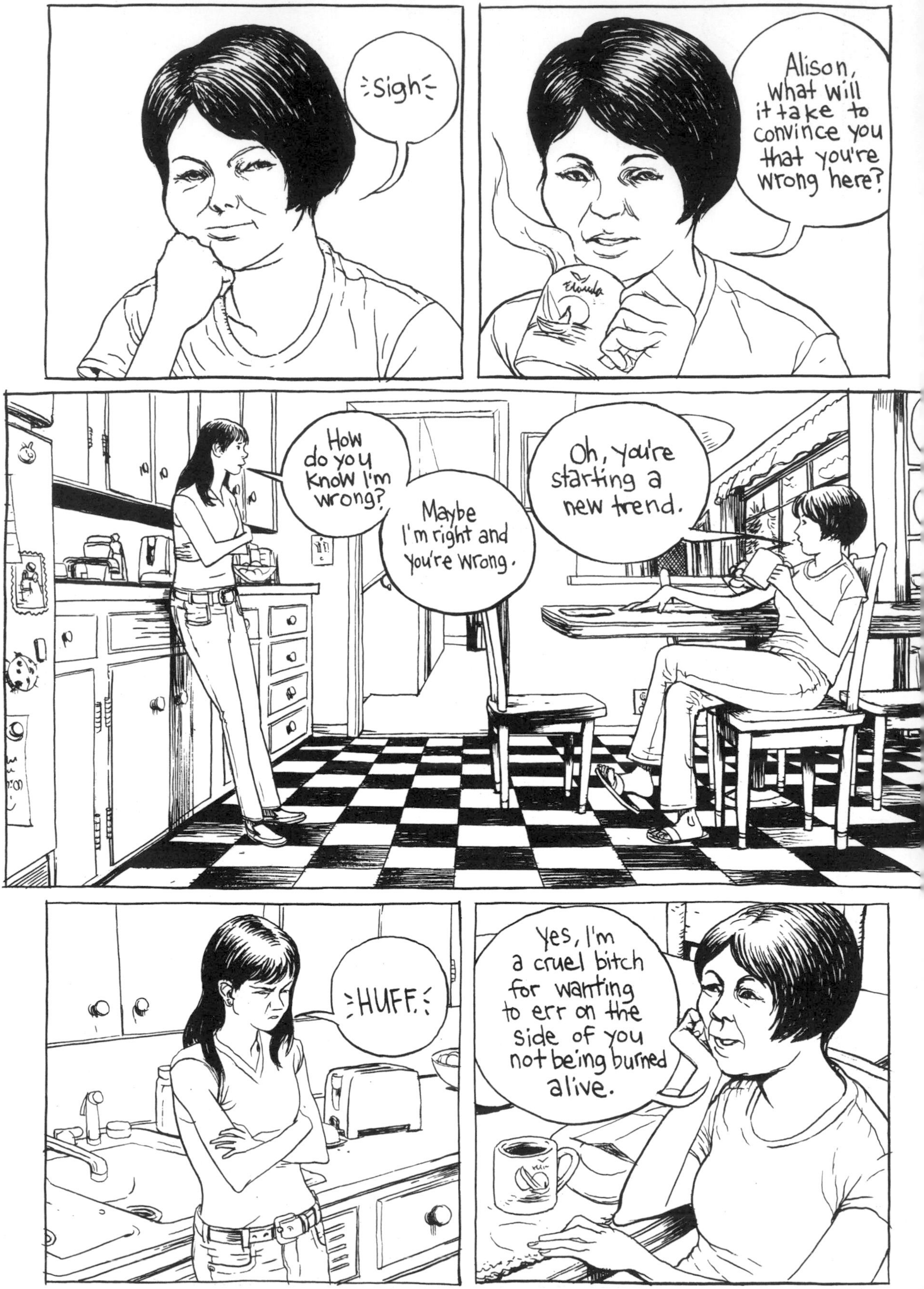
Sigh
Alison, what will it take to convince you that you're wrong here?
How do you know I'm wrong?
Maybe I'm right and you're wrong.
Oh, you're starting a new trend.
HUFF.
Yes, I'm a cruel bitch for wanting to err on the side of you not being burned alive.

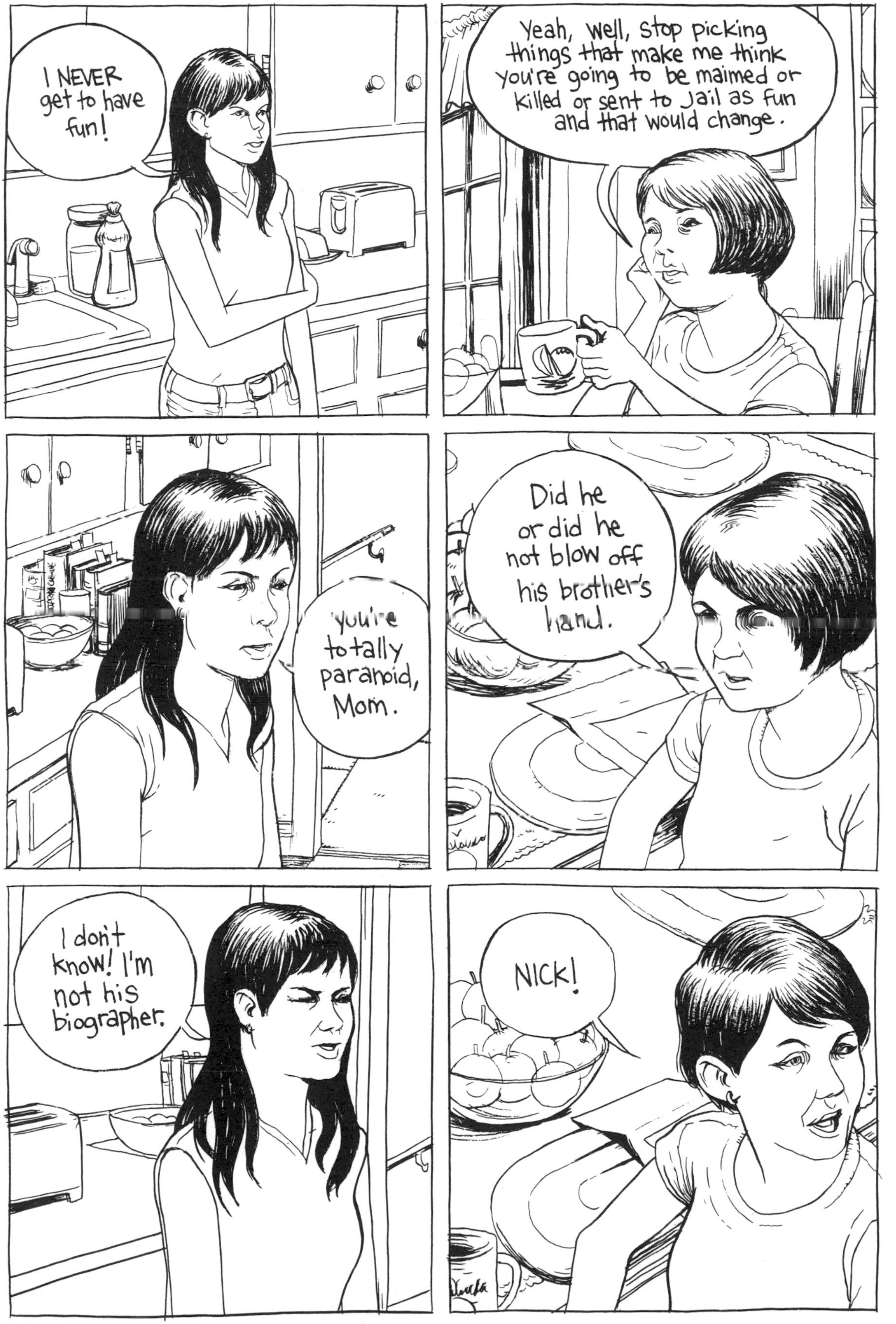
I NEVER get to have fun!
Yeah, well, stop picking things that make me think you're going to be maimed or killed or sent to jail as fun and that would change.
you're totally paranoid, Mom.
Did he or did he not blow off his brother's hand.
I don't know! I'm not his biographer.
NICK!

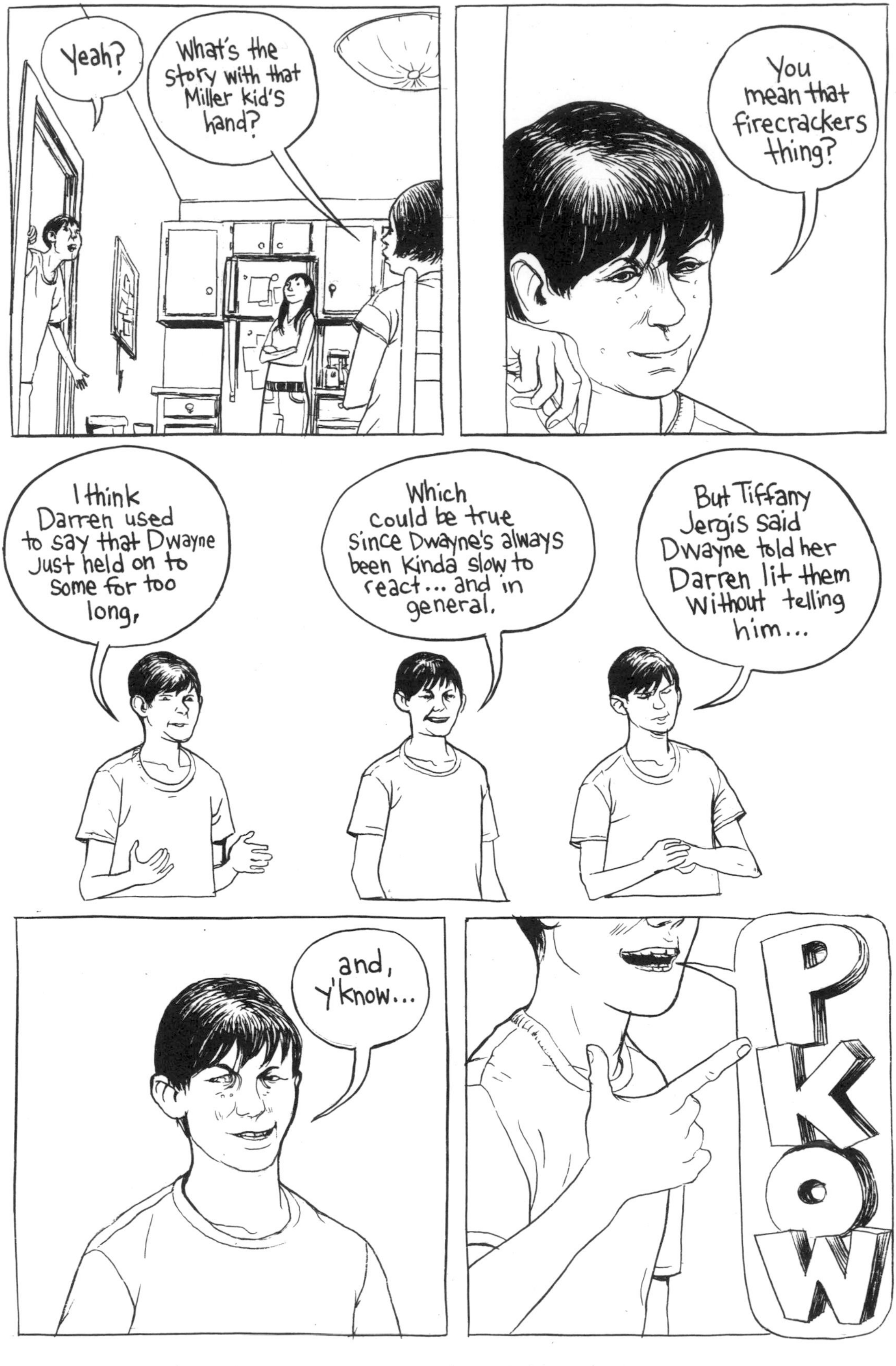

Yeah?
What's the story with that Miller kid's hand?
You mean that firecrackers thing?
I think Darren used to say that Dwayne just held on to some for too long,
Which could be true since Dwayne's always been kinda slow to react... and in general.
But Tiffany Jergis said Dwayne told her Darren lit them without telling him...
and, y'know...
PKOW

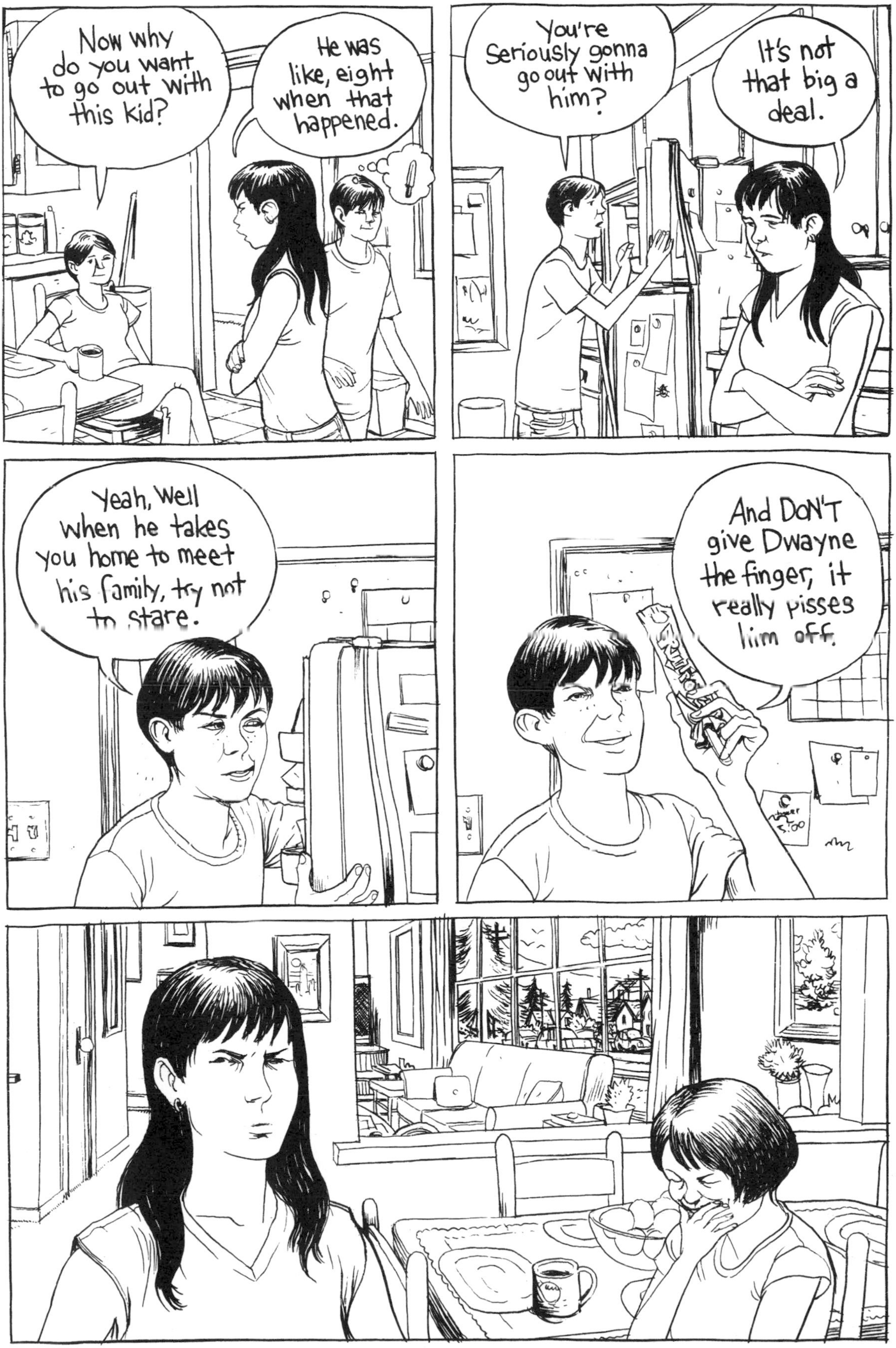
Now why do you want to go out with this kid?
He was like, eight when that happened.
You're seriously gonna go out with him?
It's not that big a deal.
Yeah, well when he takes you home to meet his family, try not to stare.
And DON'T give Dwayne the finger, it really pisses him off.

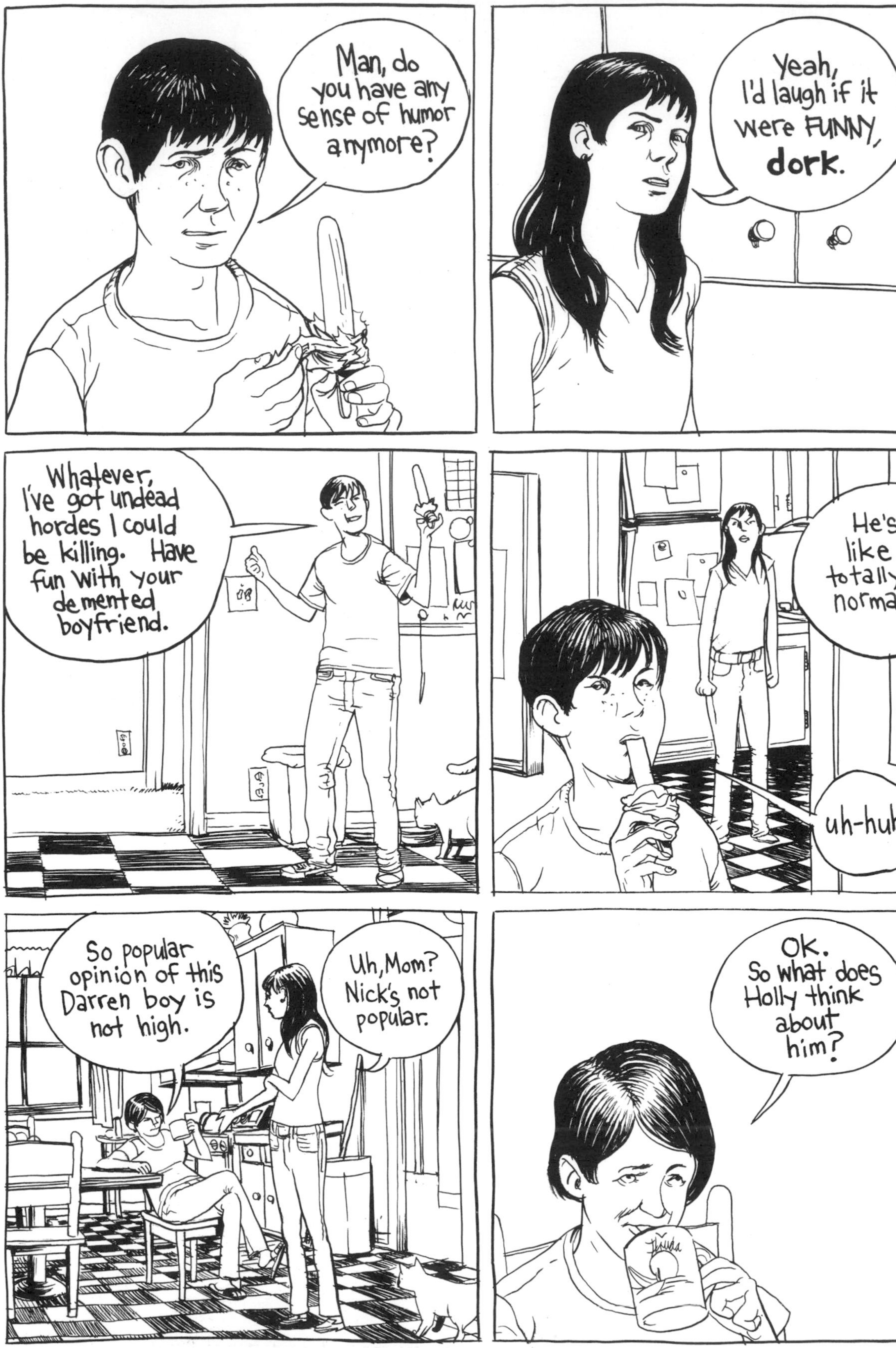
Man, do you have any sense of humor anymore?
Yeah, I'd laugh if it were FUNNY, **dork**.
Whatever, I've got undead hordes I could be killing. Have fun with your demented boyfriend.
He's like totally normal!
uh-huh.
So popular opinion of this Darren boy is not high.
Uh, Mom? Nick's not popular.
OK. So what does Holly think about him?

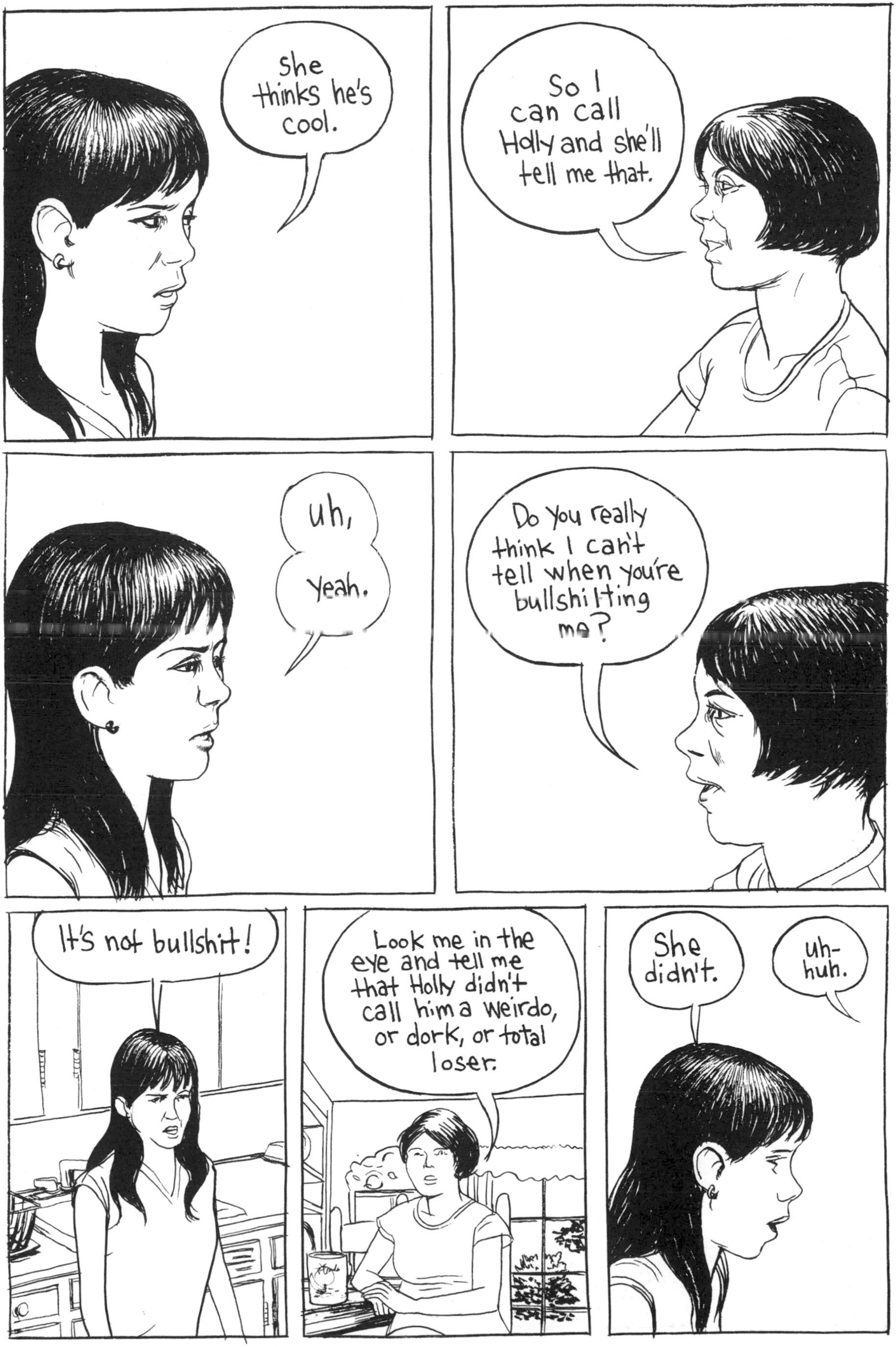
She thinks he's cool.
So I can call Holly and she'll tell me that.
uh,
Yeah.
Do you really think I can't tell when you're bullshitting me?
It's not bullshit!
Look me in the eye and tell me that Holly didn't call him a weirdo, or dork, or total loser.
She didn't.
uh-huh.

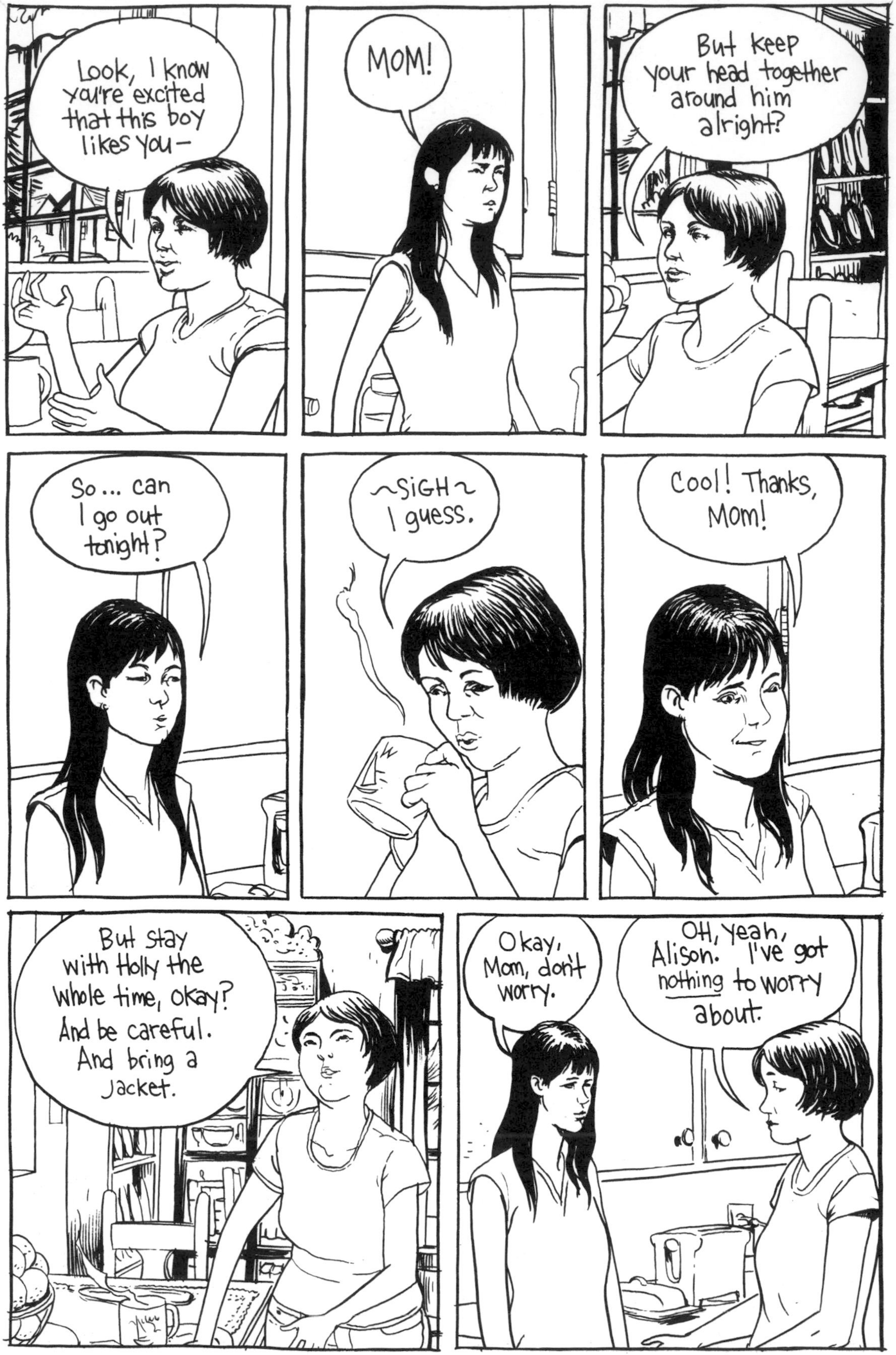
Look, I know you're excited that this boy likes you–
MOM!
But keep your head together around him alright?
So... can I go out tonight?
~SIGH~ I guess.
Cool! Thanks, Mom!
But stay with Holly the whole time, okay? And be careful. And bring a jacket.
Okay, Mom, don't worry.
OH, Yeah, Alison. I've got nothing to worry about.

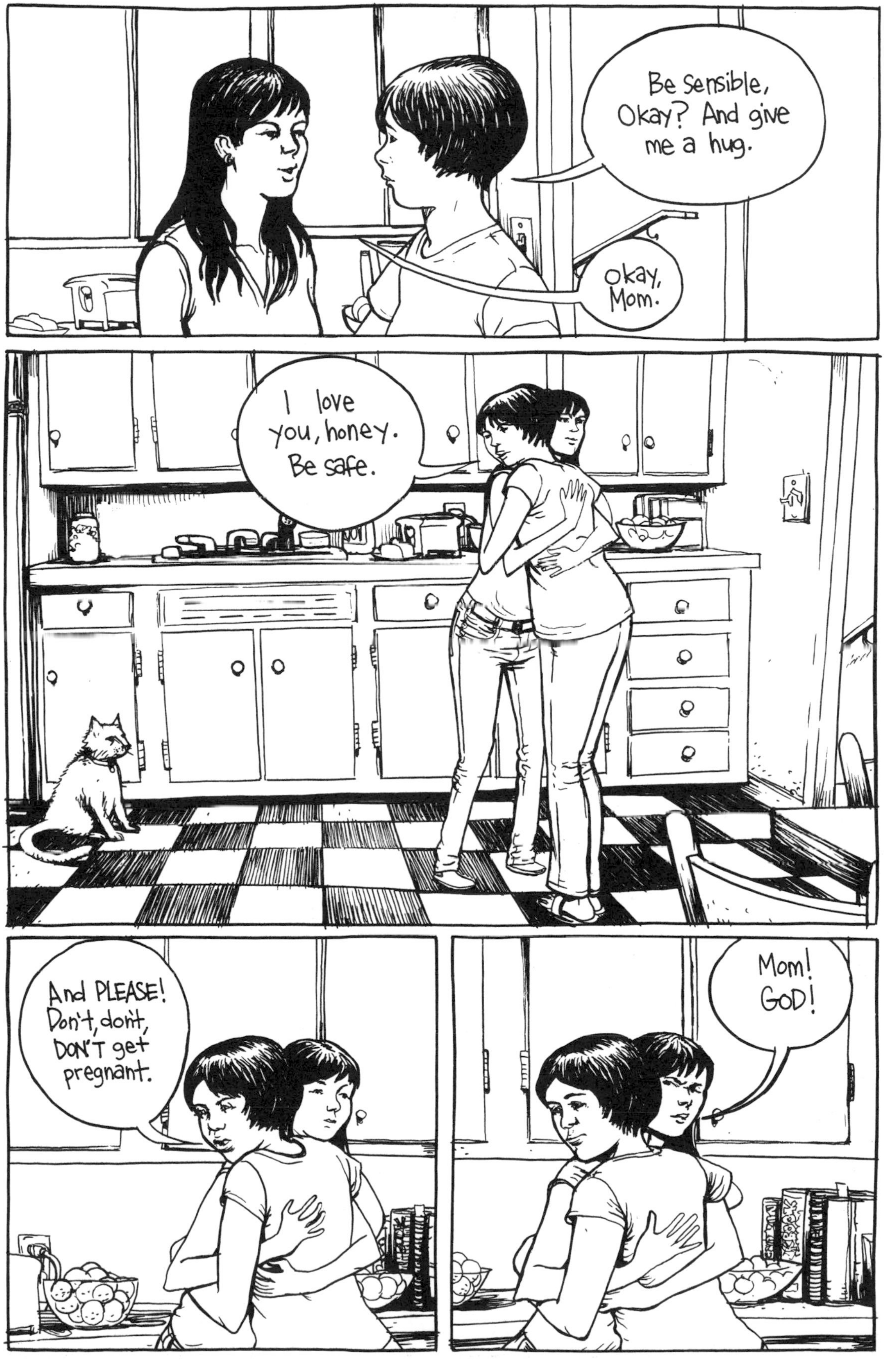
Be sensible, Okay? And give me a hug.
Okay, Mom.
I love you, honey. Be safe.
And PLEASE! Don't, don't, DON'T get pregnant.
Mom! GOD!

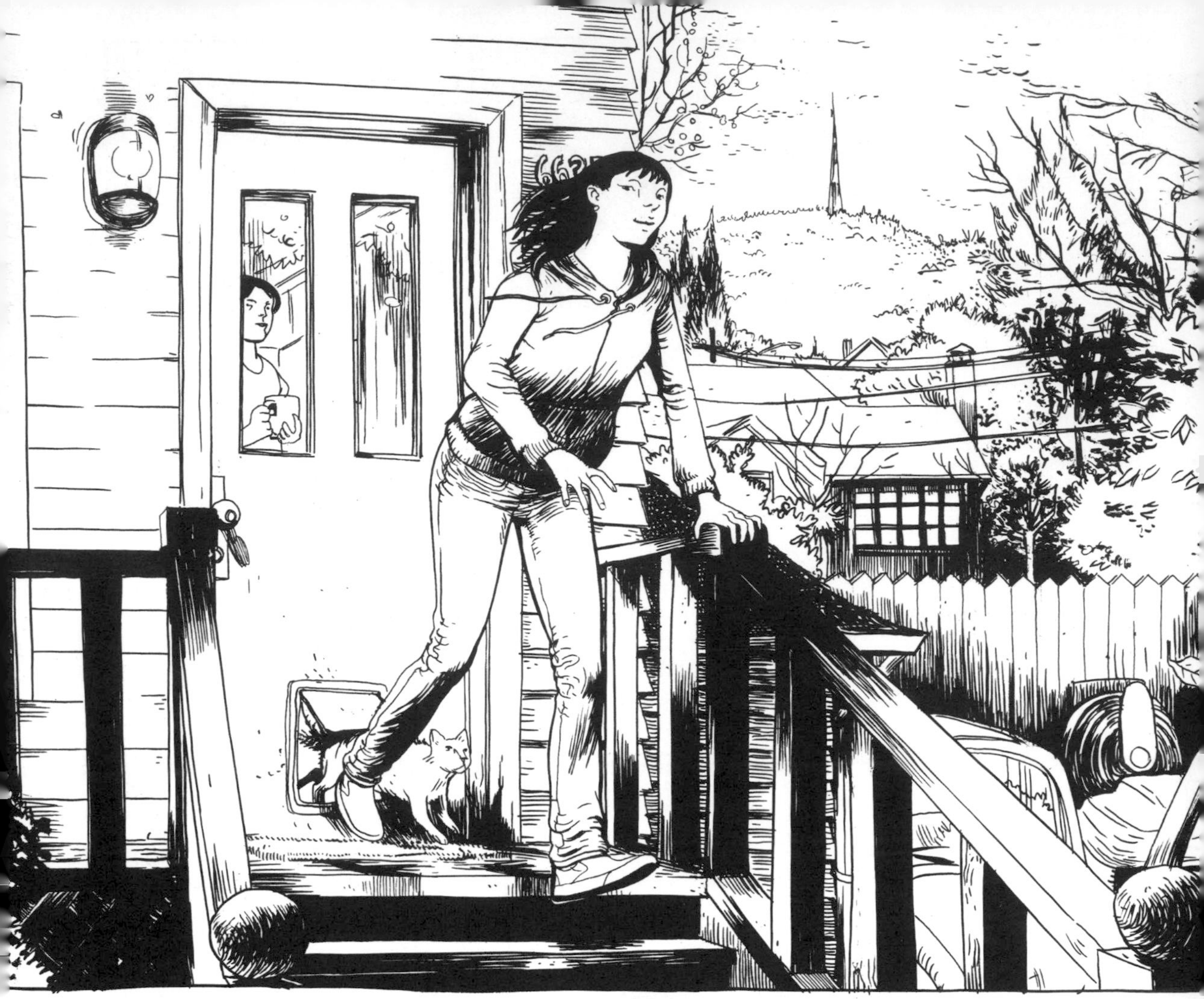

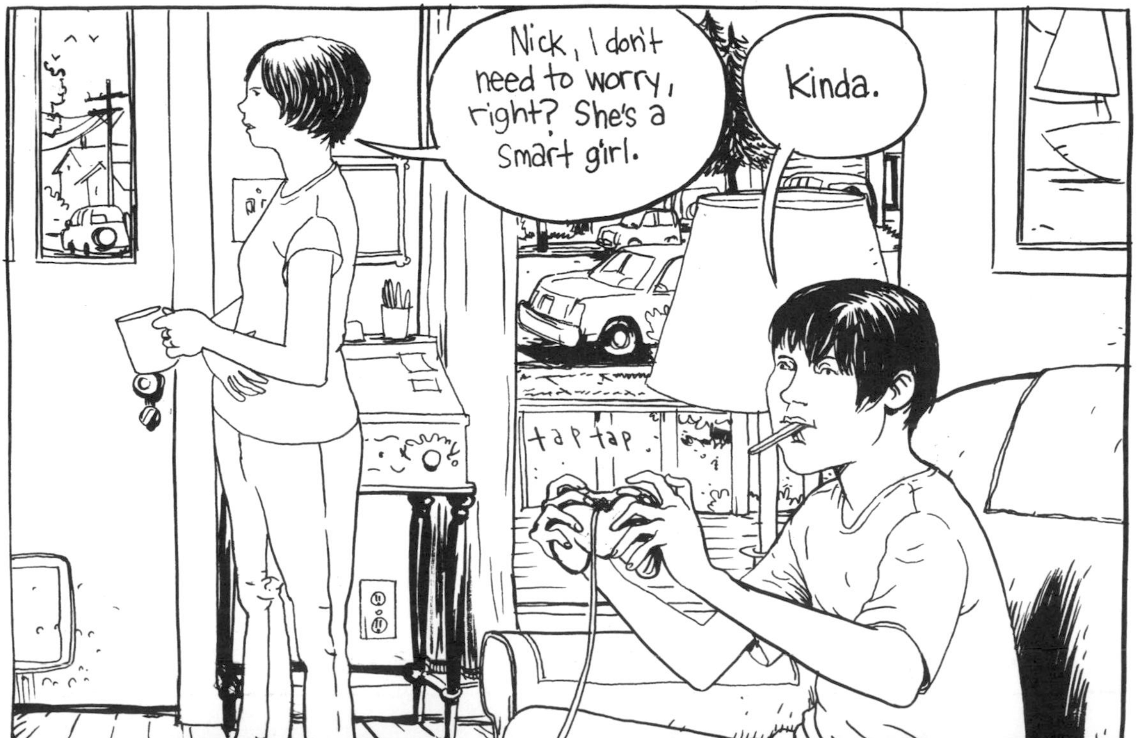
Nick, I don't need to worry, right? She's a smart girl.
Kinda.
tap tap

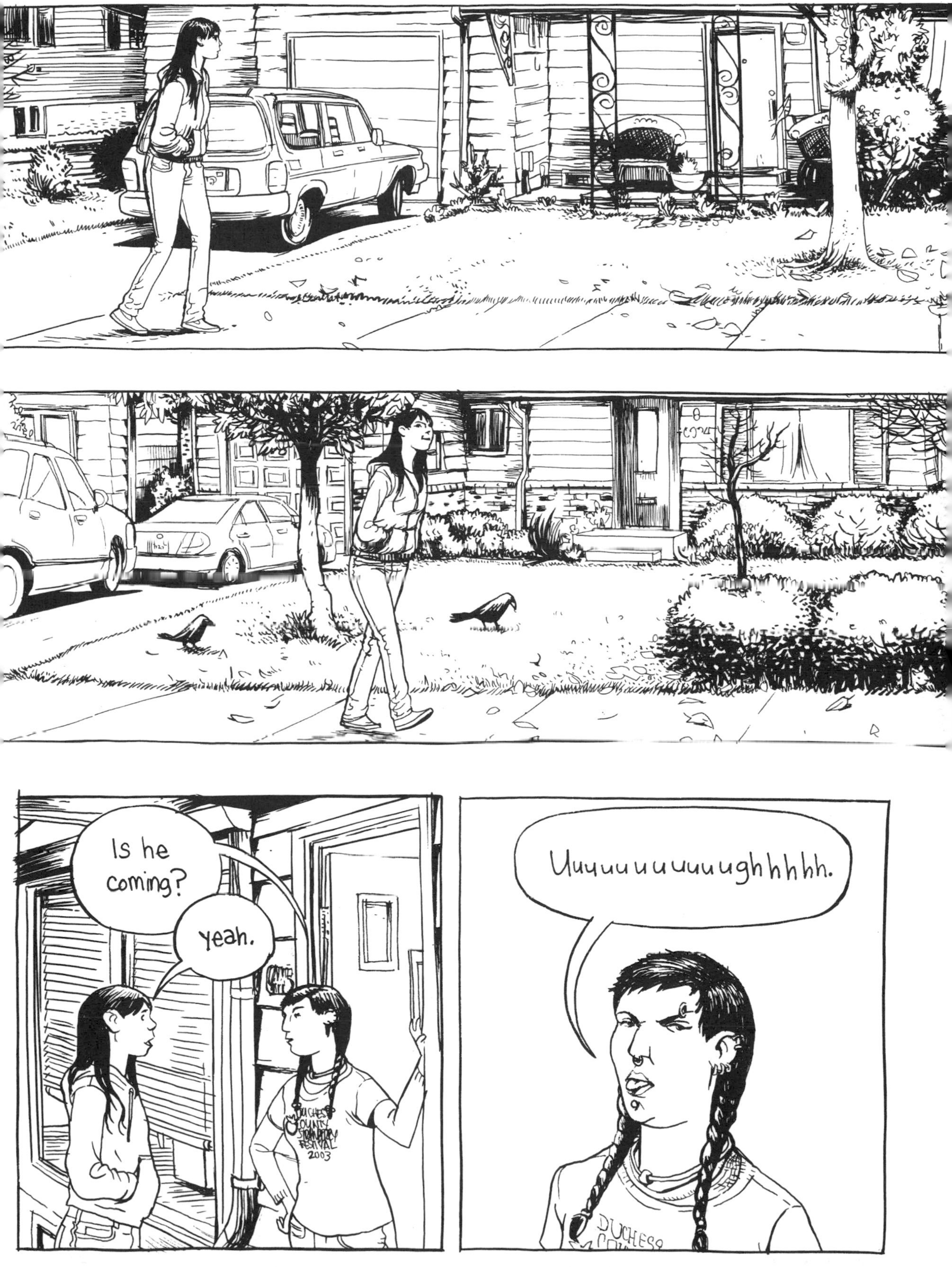
Is he coming?
yeah.
DUCHESS COUNTY STRAWBERRY FESTIVAL 2003
Uuuuuuuuuuughhhhh.

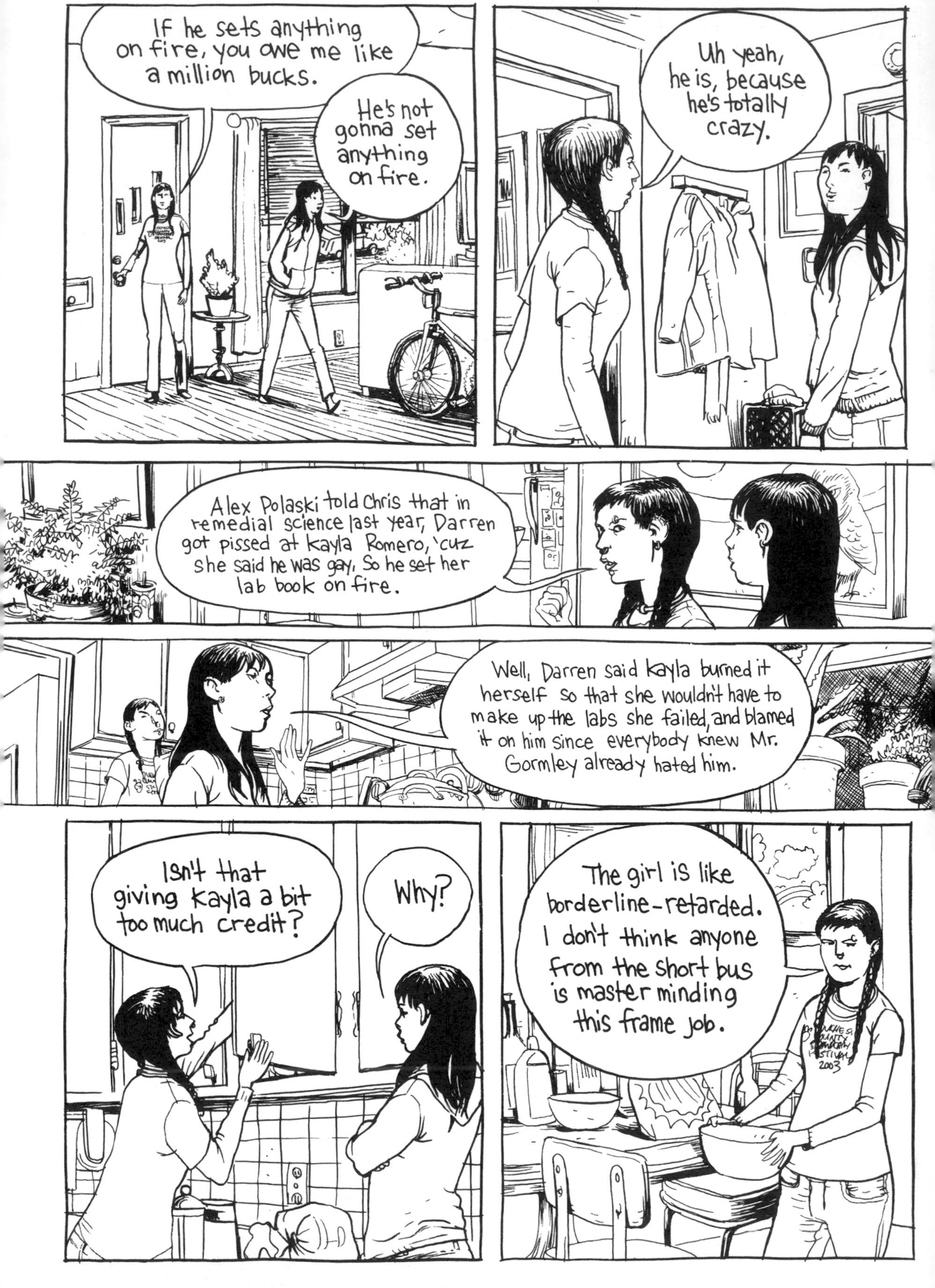
If he sets anything on fire, you owe me like a million bucks.
He's not gonna set anything on fire.
Uh yeah, he is, because he's totally crazy.
Alex Polaski told Chris that in remedial science last year, Darren got pissed at Kayla Romero, 'cuz she said he was gay, so he set her lab book on fire.
Well, Darren said Kayla burned it herself so that she wouldn't have to make up the labs she failed, and blamed it on him since everybody knew Mr. Gormley already hated him.
Isn't that giving Kayla a bit too much credit?
Why?
The girl is like borderline-retarded. I don't think anyone from the short bus is master minding this frame job.

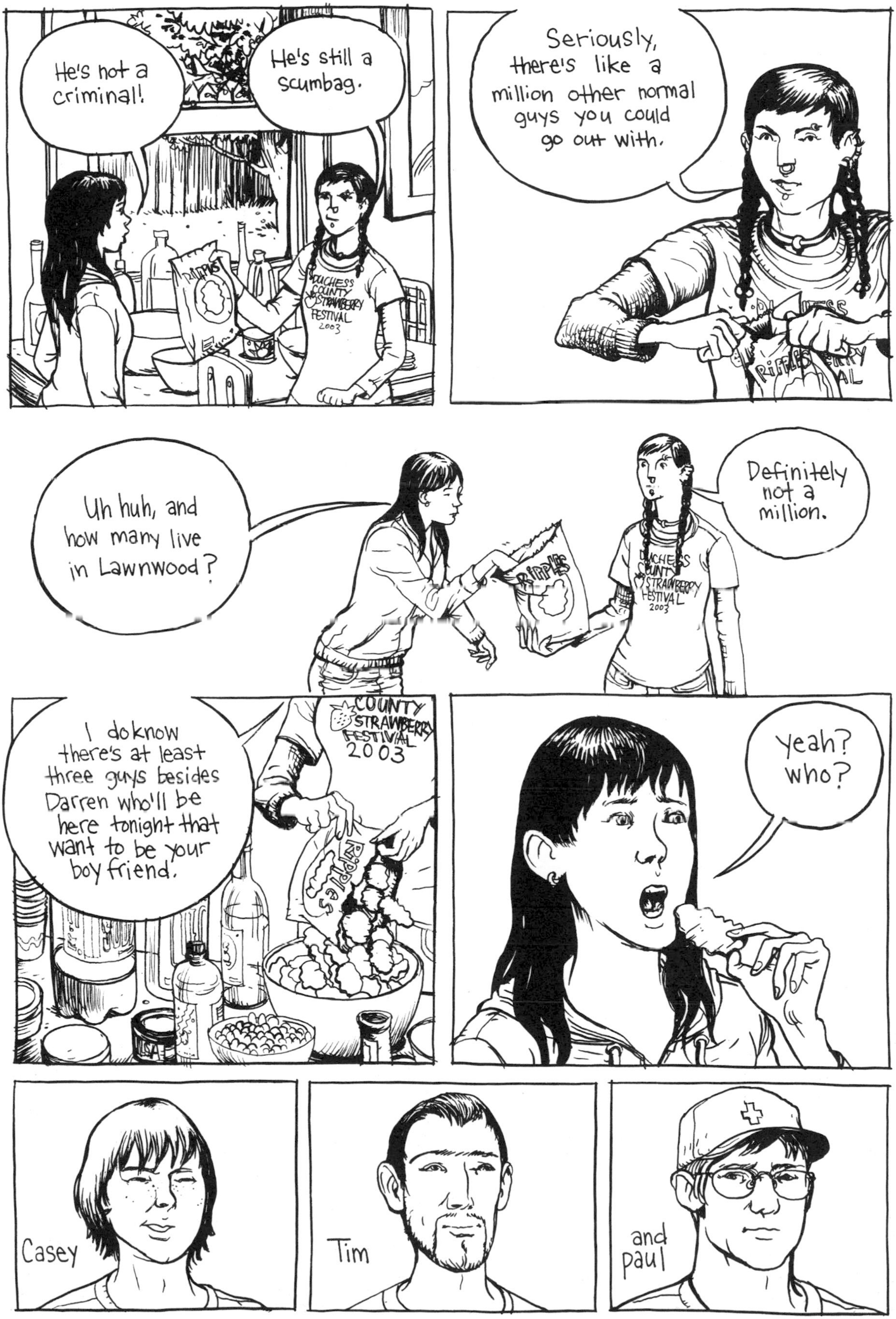
He's not a criminal!
He's still a scumbag.
RIPPLES
DUCHESS COUNTY STRAWBERRY FESTIVAL 2003
Seriously, there's like a million other normal guys you could go out with.
Uh huh, and how many live in Lawnwood?
Definitely not a million.
I do know there's at least three guys besides Darren who'll be here tonight that want to be your boy friend.
COUNTY STRAWBERRY FESTIVAL 2003
Yeah? who?
Casey
Tim
and paul

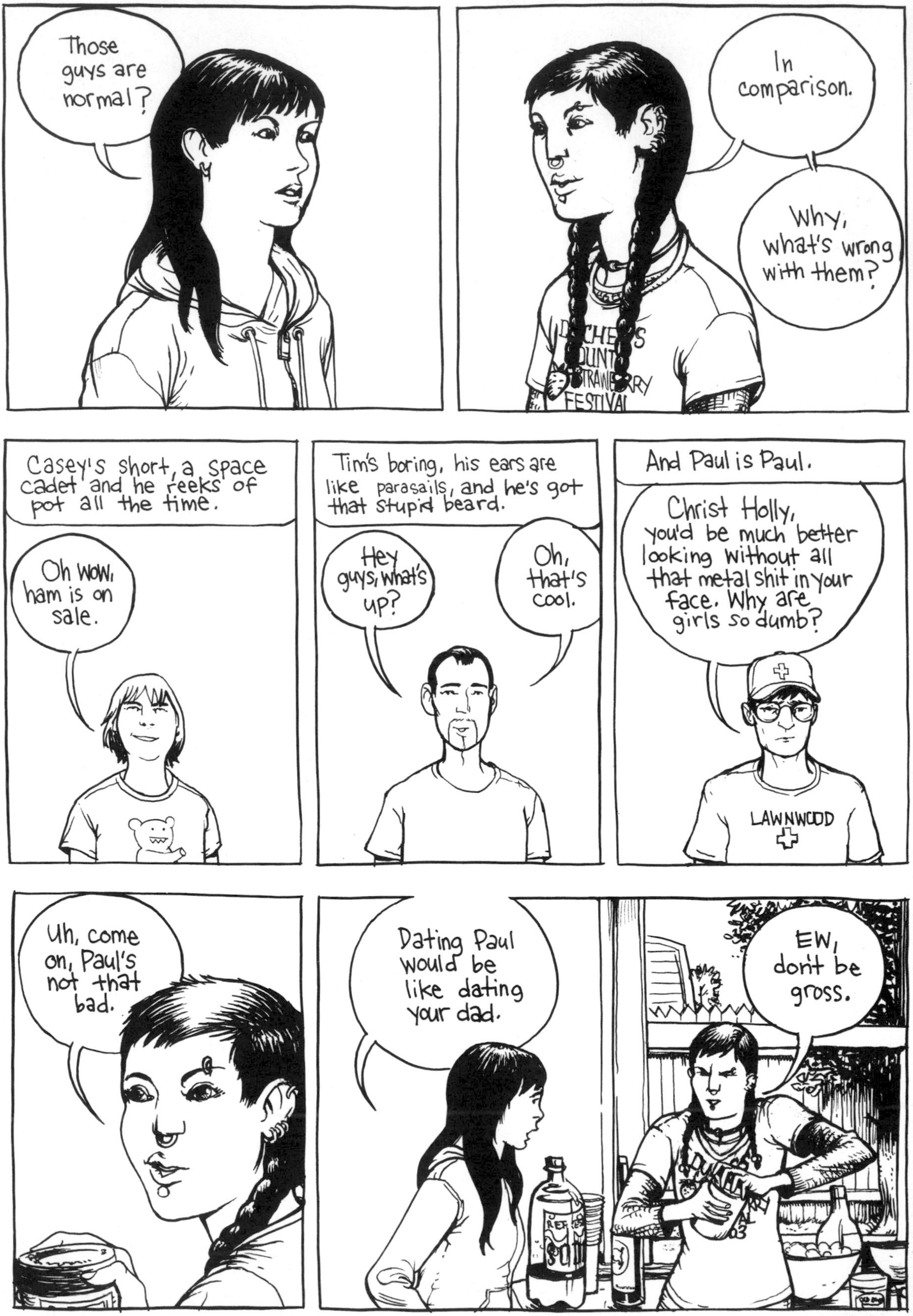
Those guys are normal?
In comparison.
Why, what's wrong with them?
Casey's short, a space cadet and he reeks of pot all the time.
Oh wow, ham is on sale.
Tim's boring, his ears are like parasails, and he's got that stupid beard.
Hey guys, what's up?
Oh, that's cool.
And Paul is Paul.
Christ Holly, you'd be much better looking without all that metal shit in your face. Why are girls so dumb?
LAWNWOOD
Uh, come on, Paul's not that bad.
Dating Paul would be like dating your dad.
EW, don't be gross.

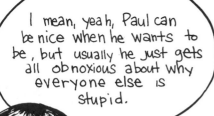

I mean, yeah, Paul can be nice when he wants to be, but usually he just gets all obnoxious about why everyone else is stupid.

BingBang

Otherwise he just drones on about being a Junior EMT, but like, whatever! He's a glorified candy striper.

Yeah, he's such a dick for trying to help people.

Can you get that?

Hey, Alison.

Hey.

Hey Allison! What's up?

Hey guys.

Holly's in the kitchen.

Oh my god, I have to go tell her what Tara did in home ec.

So... What's up?

Umm... nothin' really...

Yeah.... that's cool.

Yeah...

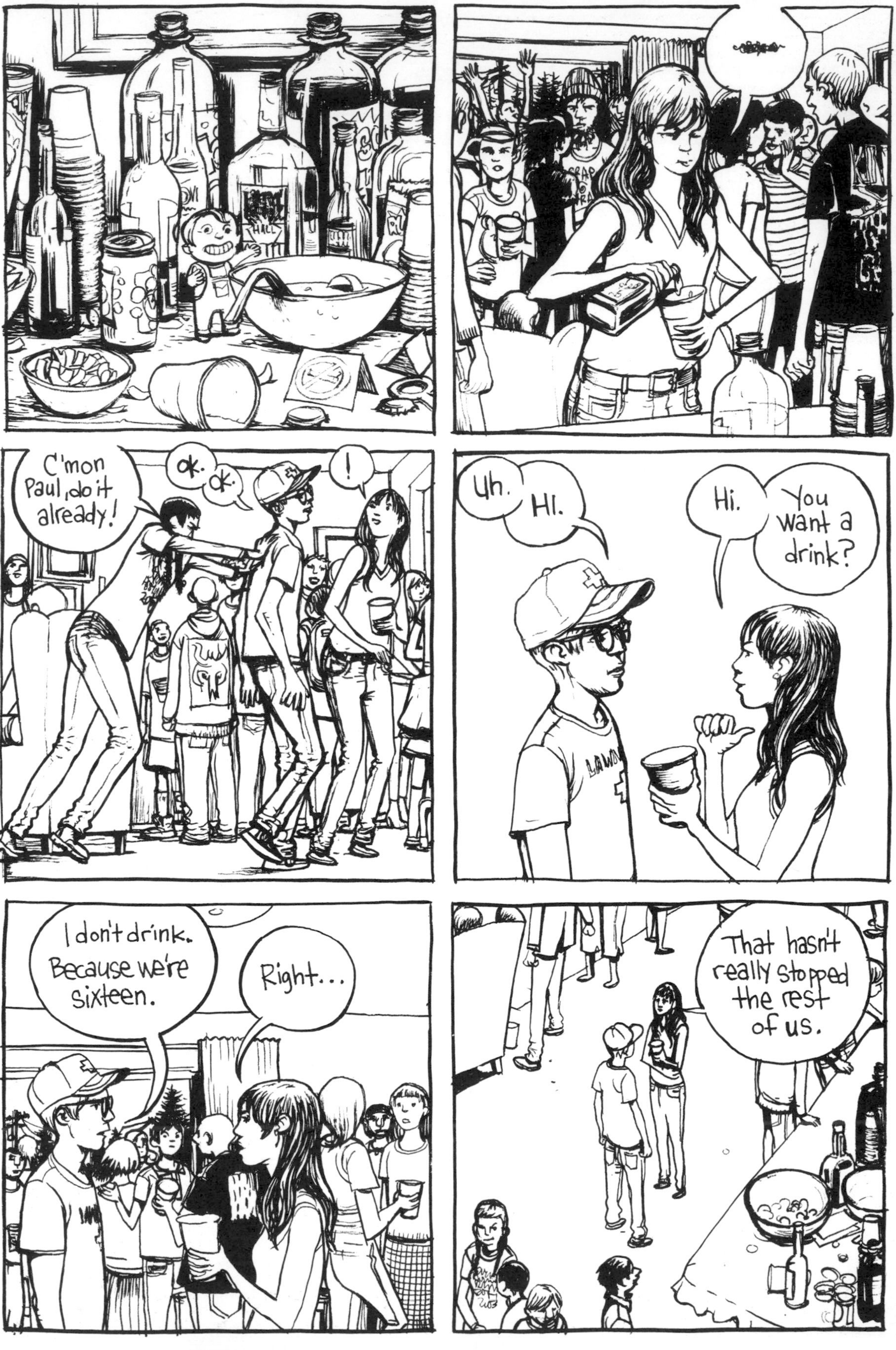
C'mon Paul, do it already!
ok. ok.
!
Uh. HI.
Hi.
You want a drink?
I don't drink. Because we're sixteen.
Right...
That hasn't really stopped the rest of us.

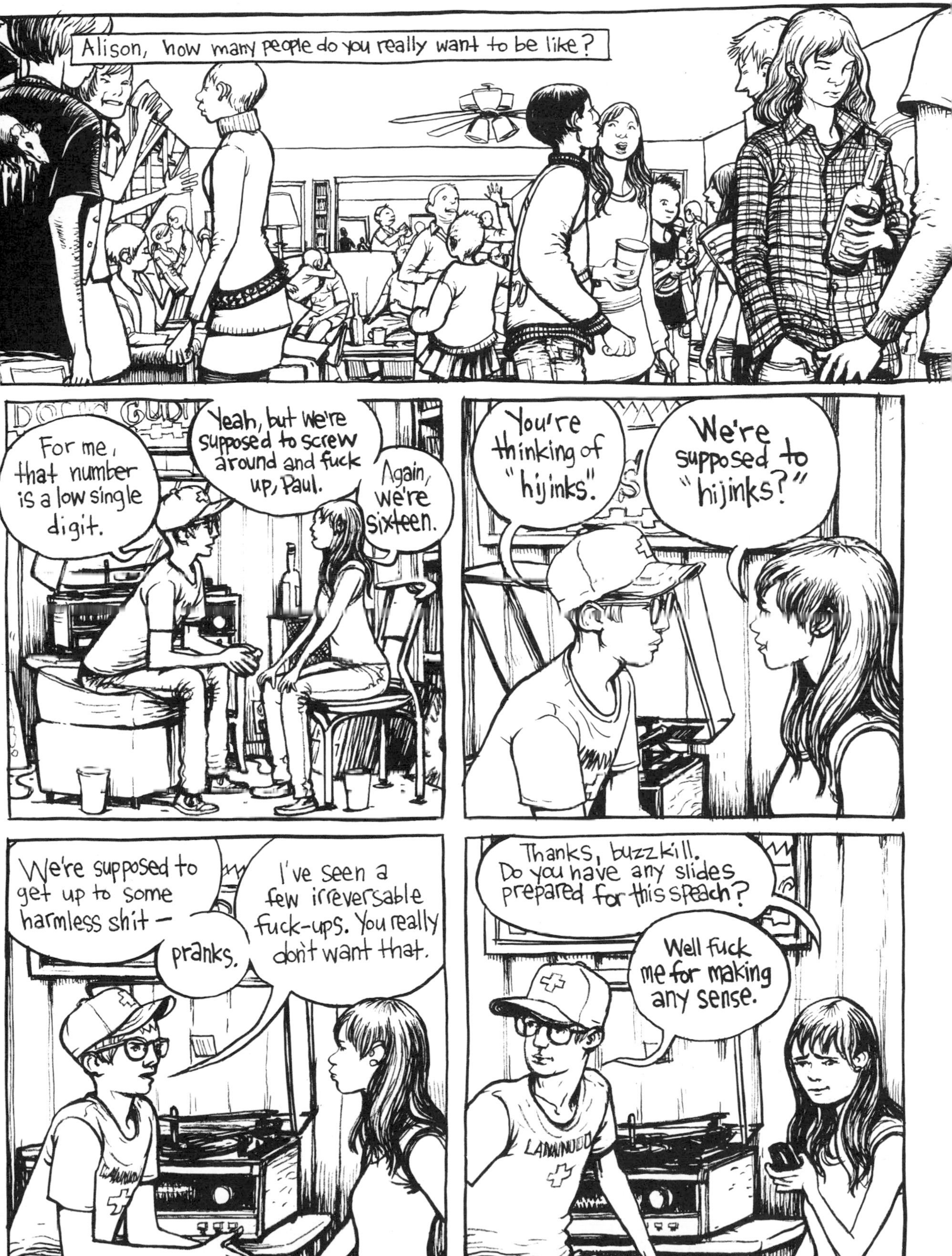
Alison, how many people do you really want to be like?
For me, that number is a low single digit.
Yeah, but we're supposed to screw around and fuck up, Paul.
Again, we're sixteen.
You're thinking of "hijinks".
We're supposed to "hijinks?"
We're supposed to get up to some harmless shit —
pranks.
I've seen a few irreversable fuck-ups. You really don't want that.
Thanks, buzzkill. Do you have any slides prepared for this speach?
Well fuck me for making any sense.

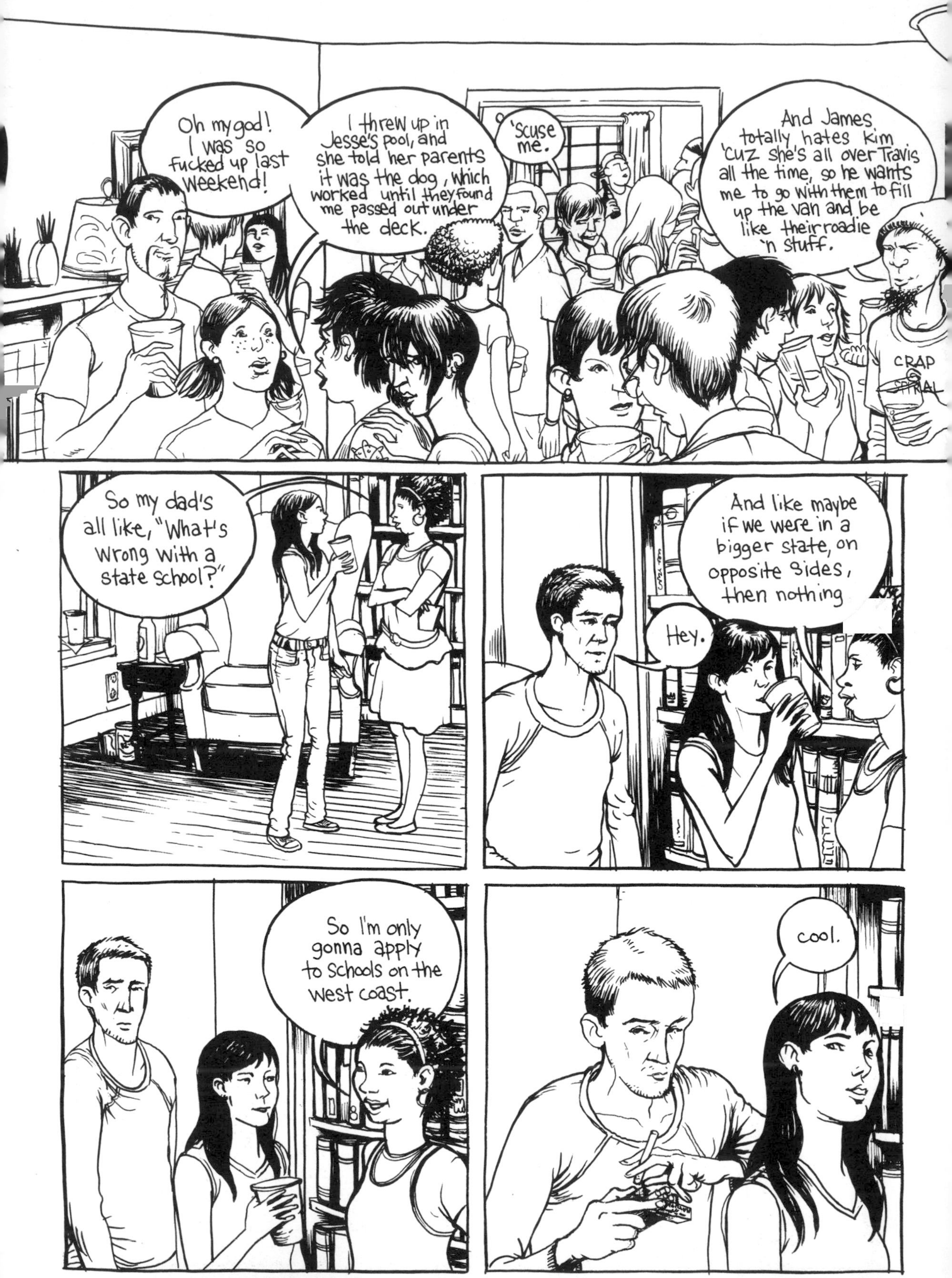
Oh my god! I was so fucked up last weekend!
I threw up in Jesse's pool, and she told her parents it was the dog, which worked until they found me passed out under the deck.
'Scuse me.
And James totally hates Kim 'cuz she's all over Travis all the time, so he wants me to go with them to fill up the van and be like their roadie 'n stuff.
CRAP
So my dad's all like, "What's wrong with a state school?"
And like maybe if we were in a bigger state, on opposite sides, then nothing
Hey.
So I'm only gonna apply to schools on the west coast.
cool.

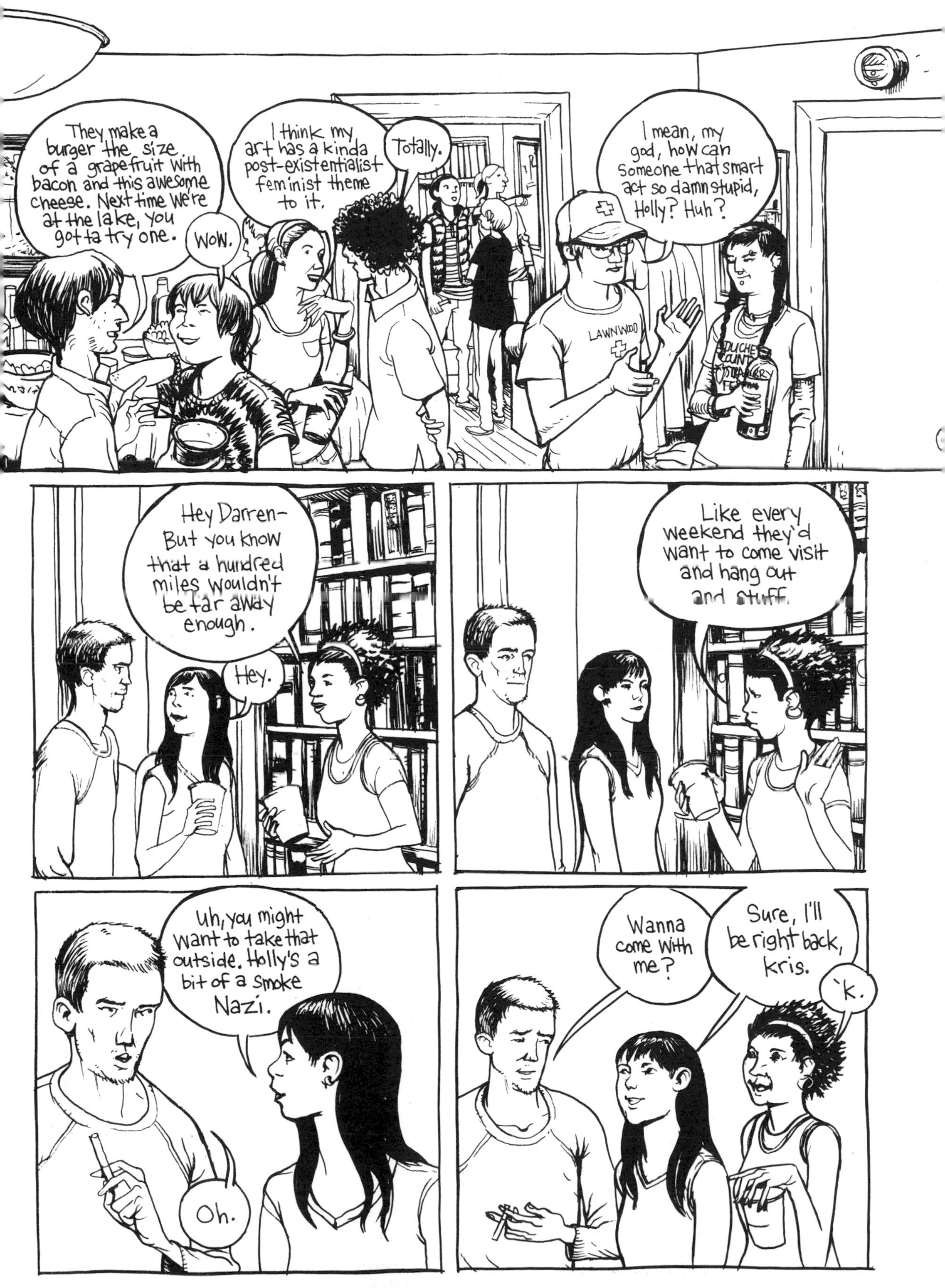

They make a burger the size of a grapefruit with bacon and this awesome cheese. Next time we're at the lake, you gotta try one.
Wow.
I think my art has a kinda post-existentialist feminist theme to it.
Totally.
I mean, my god, how can someone that smart act so damn stupid, Holly? Huh?
LAWNWOOD
Hey Darren- But you know that a hundred miles wouldn't be far away enough.
Hey.
Like every weekend they'd want to come visit and hang out and stuff.
Uh, you might want to take that outside. Holly's a bit of a smoke Nazi.
Oh.
Wanna come with me?
Sure, I'll be right back, kris.
`k.

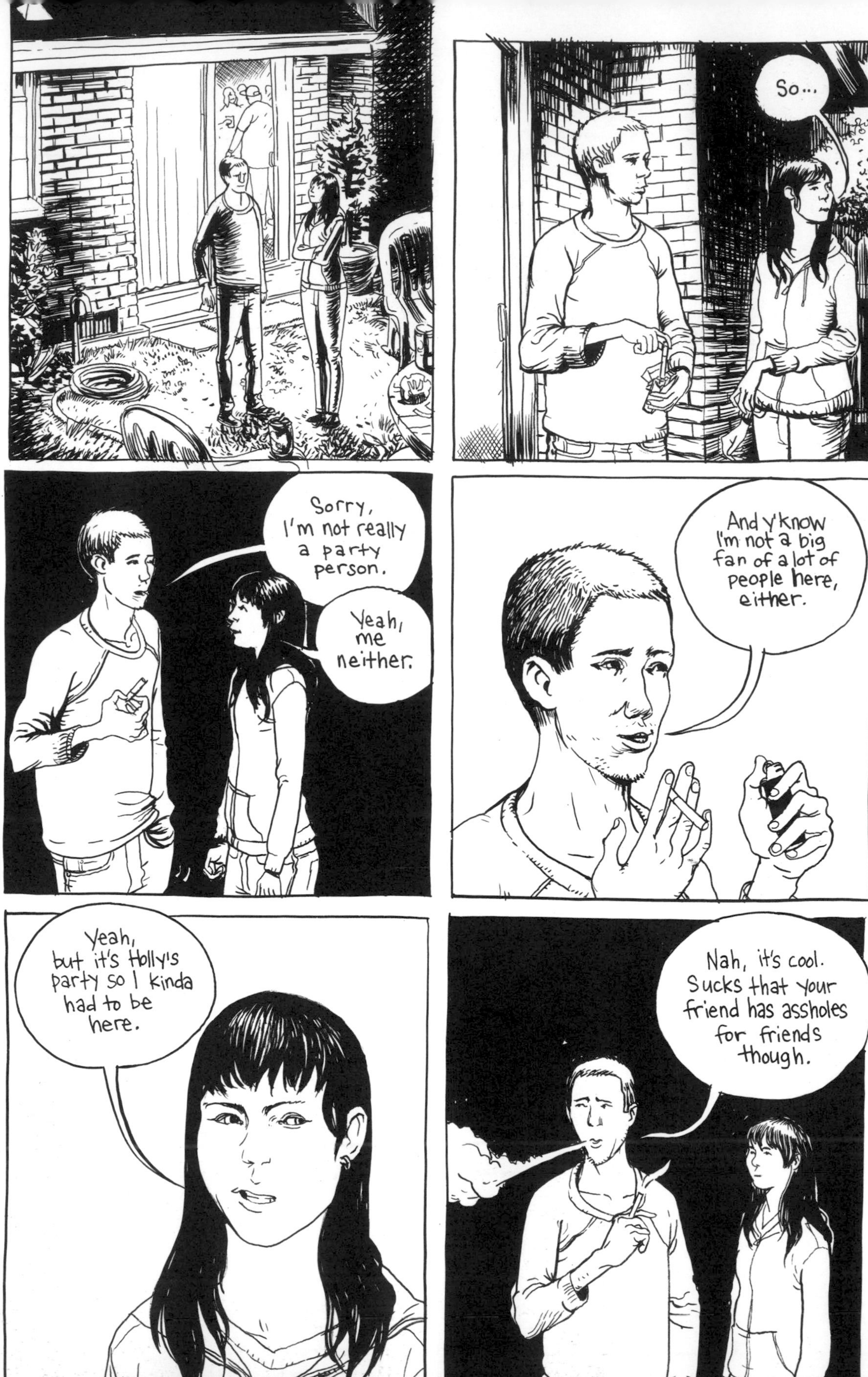
So...
Sorry, I'm not really a party person.
Yeah, me neither.
And y'know I'm not a big fan of a lot of people here, either.
Yeah, but it's Holly's party so I kinda had to be here.
Nah, it's cool. Sucks that your friend has assholes for friends though.

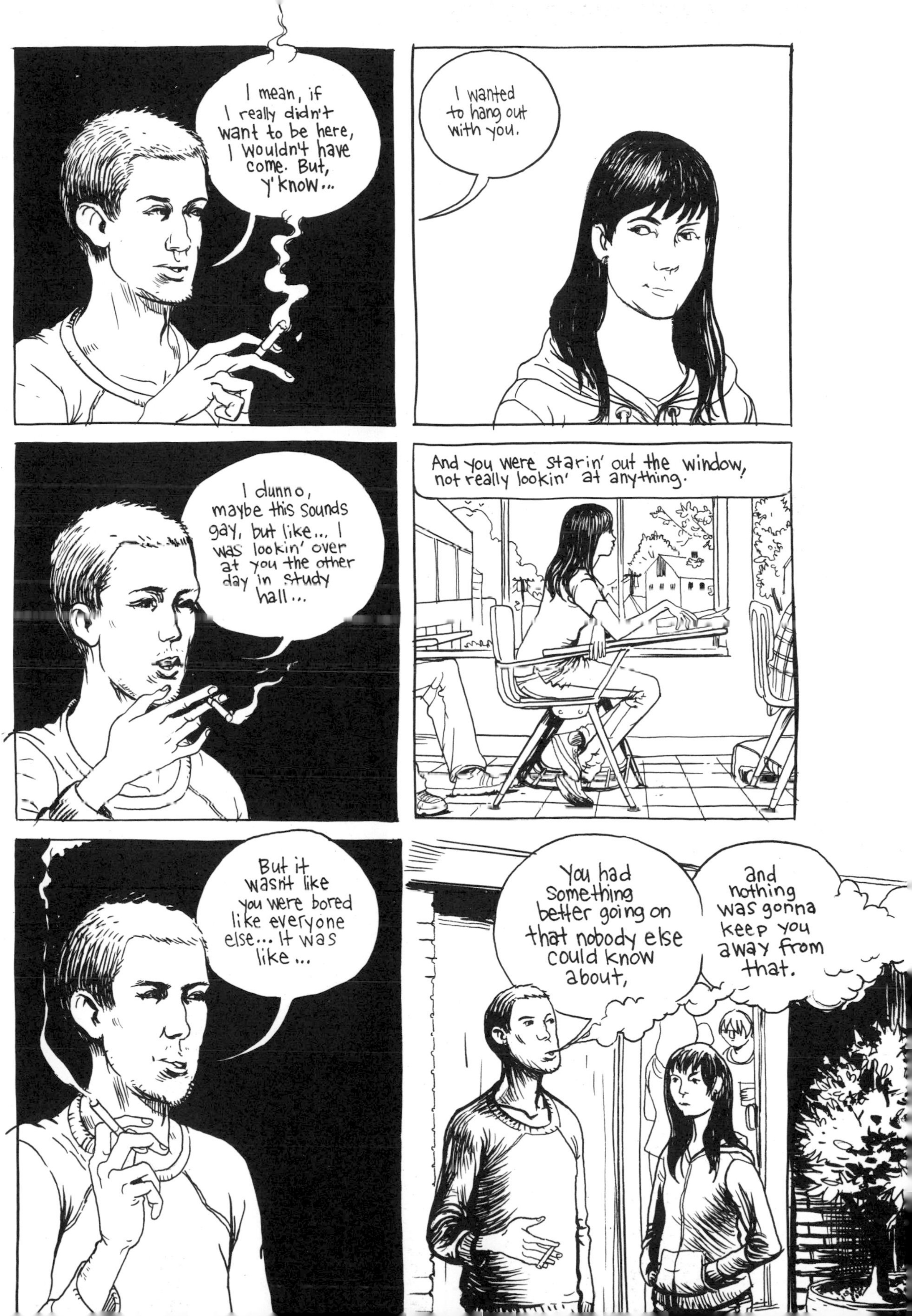
I mean, if I really didn't want to be here, I wouldn't have come. But, y'know...
I wanted to hang out with you.
I dunno, maybe this sounds gay, but like... I was lookin' over at you the other day in study hall...
And you were starin' out the window, not really lookin' at anything.
But it wasn't like you were bored like everyone else... It was like...
You had something better going on that nobody else could know about,
and nothing was gonna keep you away from that.

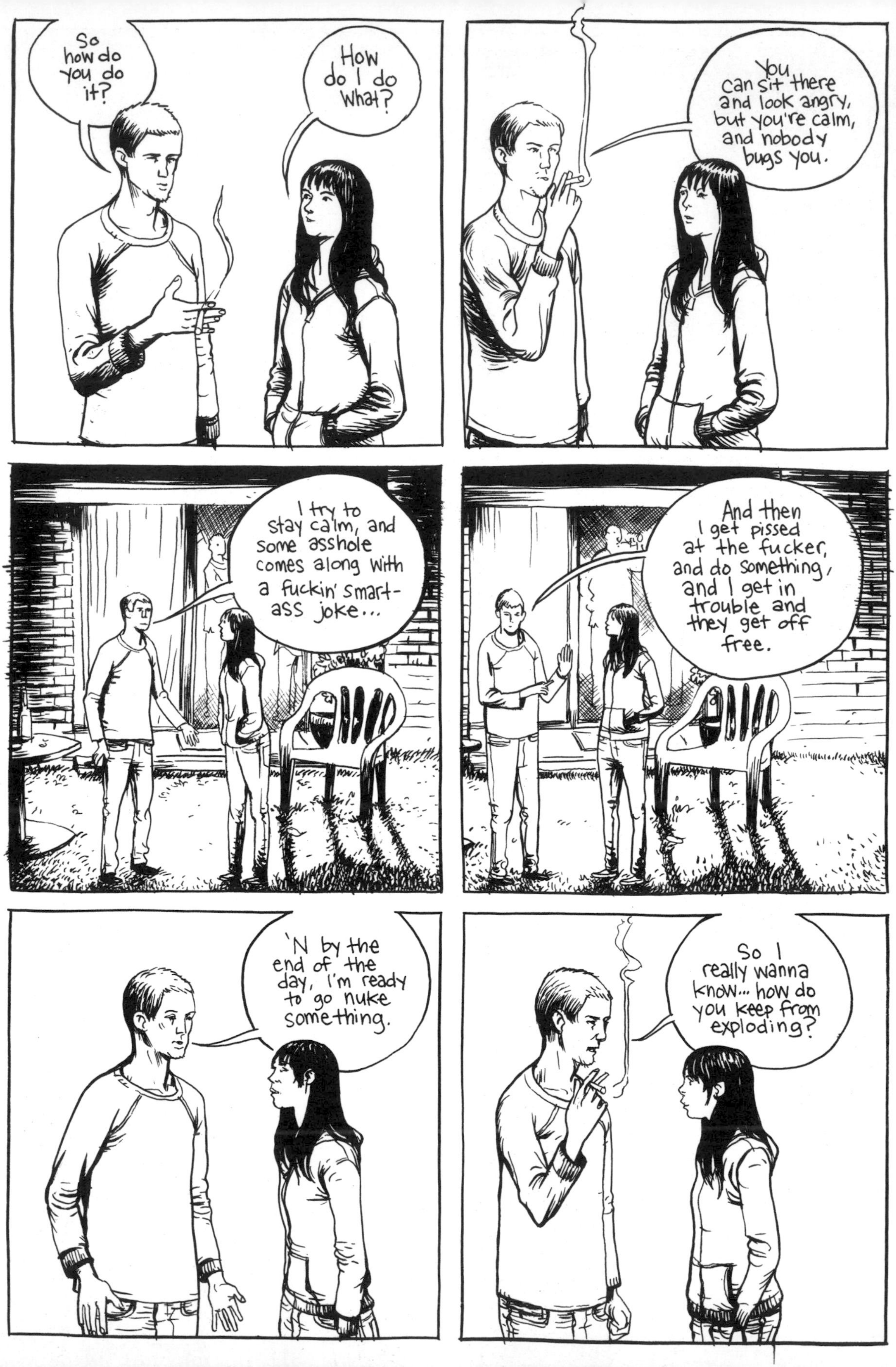
So how do you do it?
How do I do what?
You can sit there and look angry, but you're calm, and nobody bugs you.
I try to stay calm, and some asshole comes along with a fuckin' smart-ass joke...
And then I get pissed at the fucker, and do something, and I get in trouble and they get off free.
'N by the end of the day, I'm ready to go nuke something.
So I really wanna know... how do you keep from exploding?

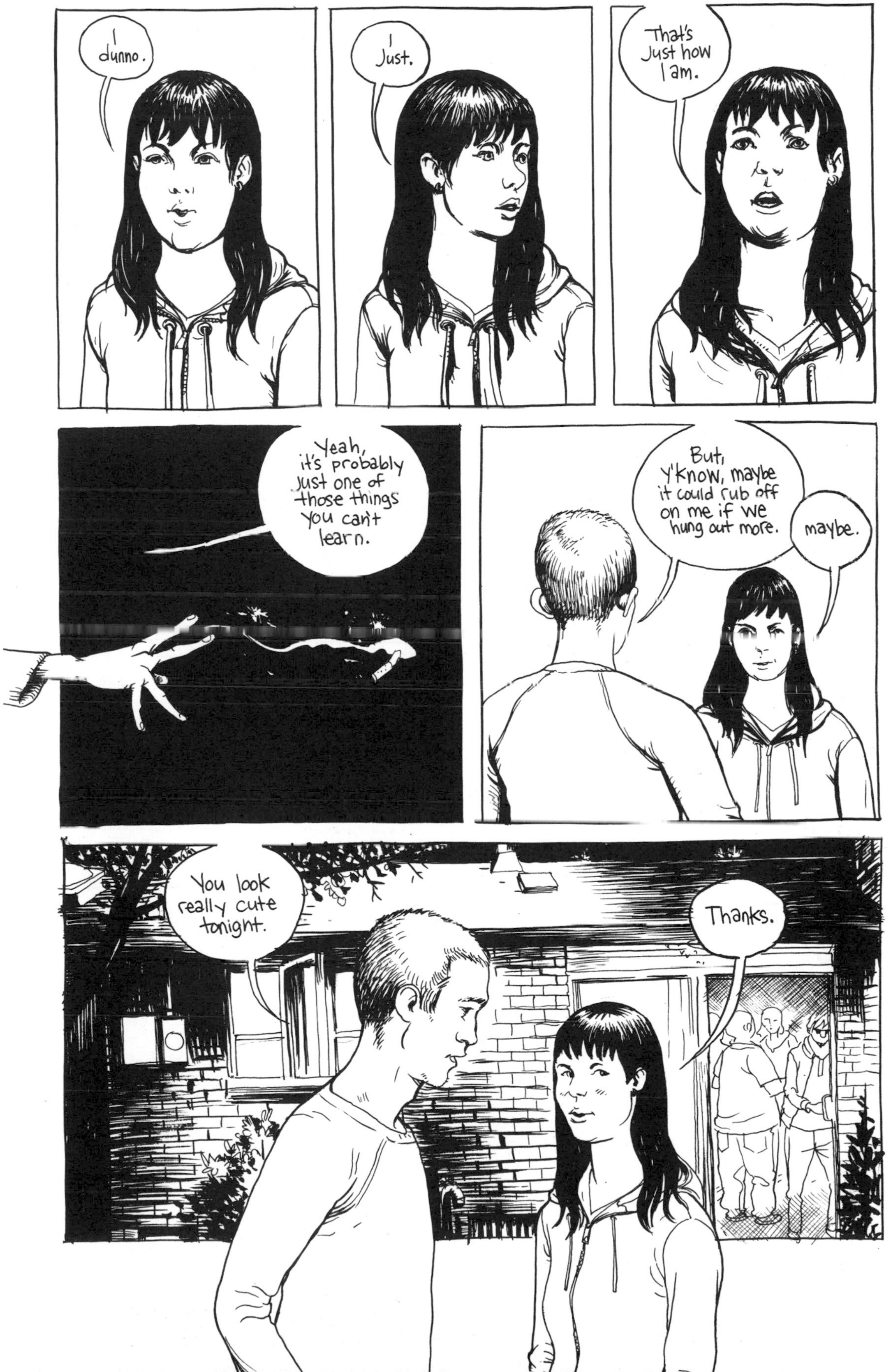
I dunno.
I just.
That's just how I am.
Yeah, it's probably just one of those things you can't learn.
But, y'know, maybe it could rub off on me if we hung out more.
maybe.
You look really cute tonight.
Thanks.

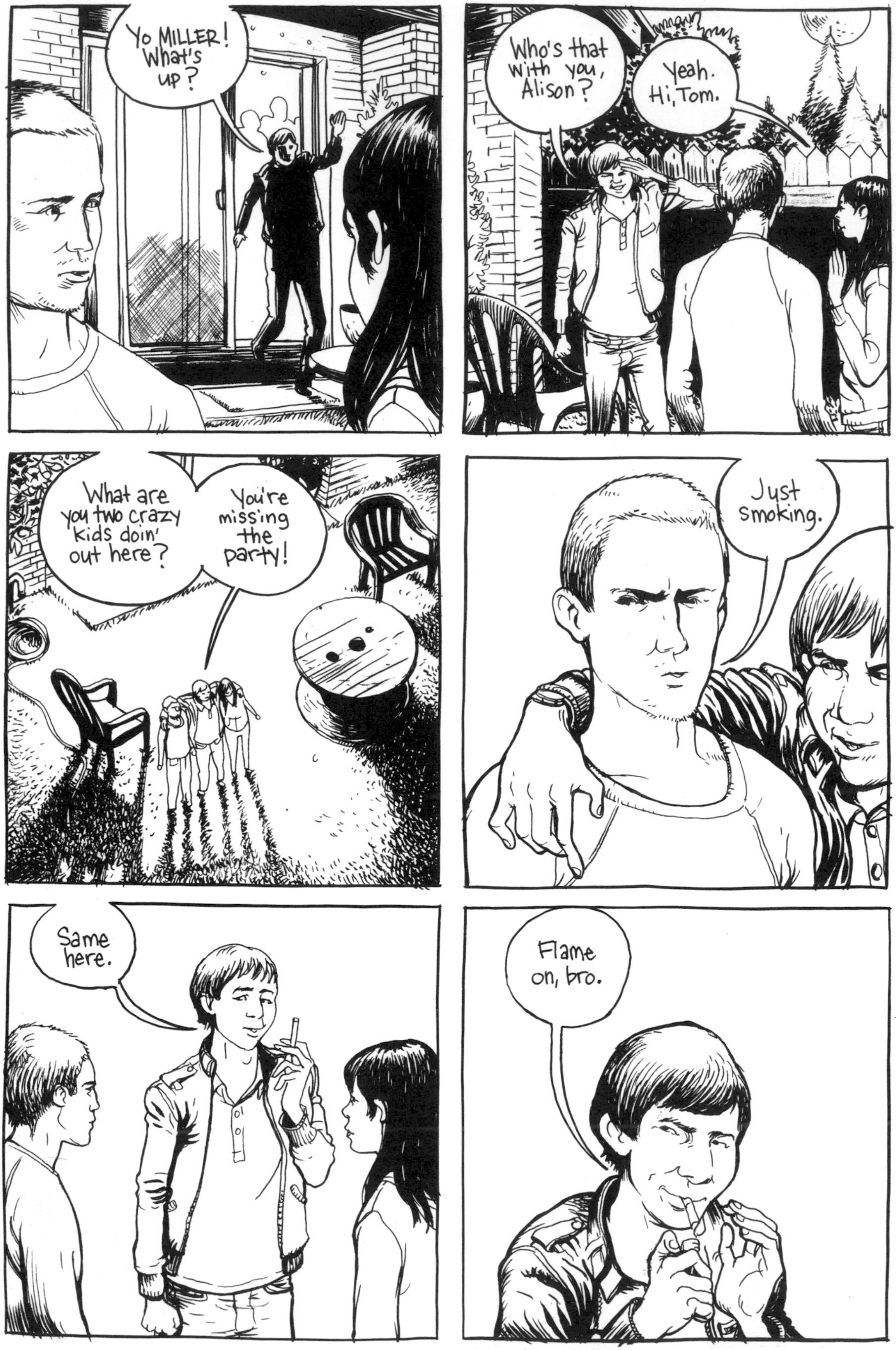
Yo MILLER! What's up?
Who's that with you, Alison?
Yeah. Hi, Tom.
What are you two crazy kids doin' out here?
You're missing the party!
Just smoking.
Same here.
Flame on, bro.

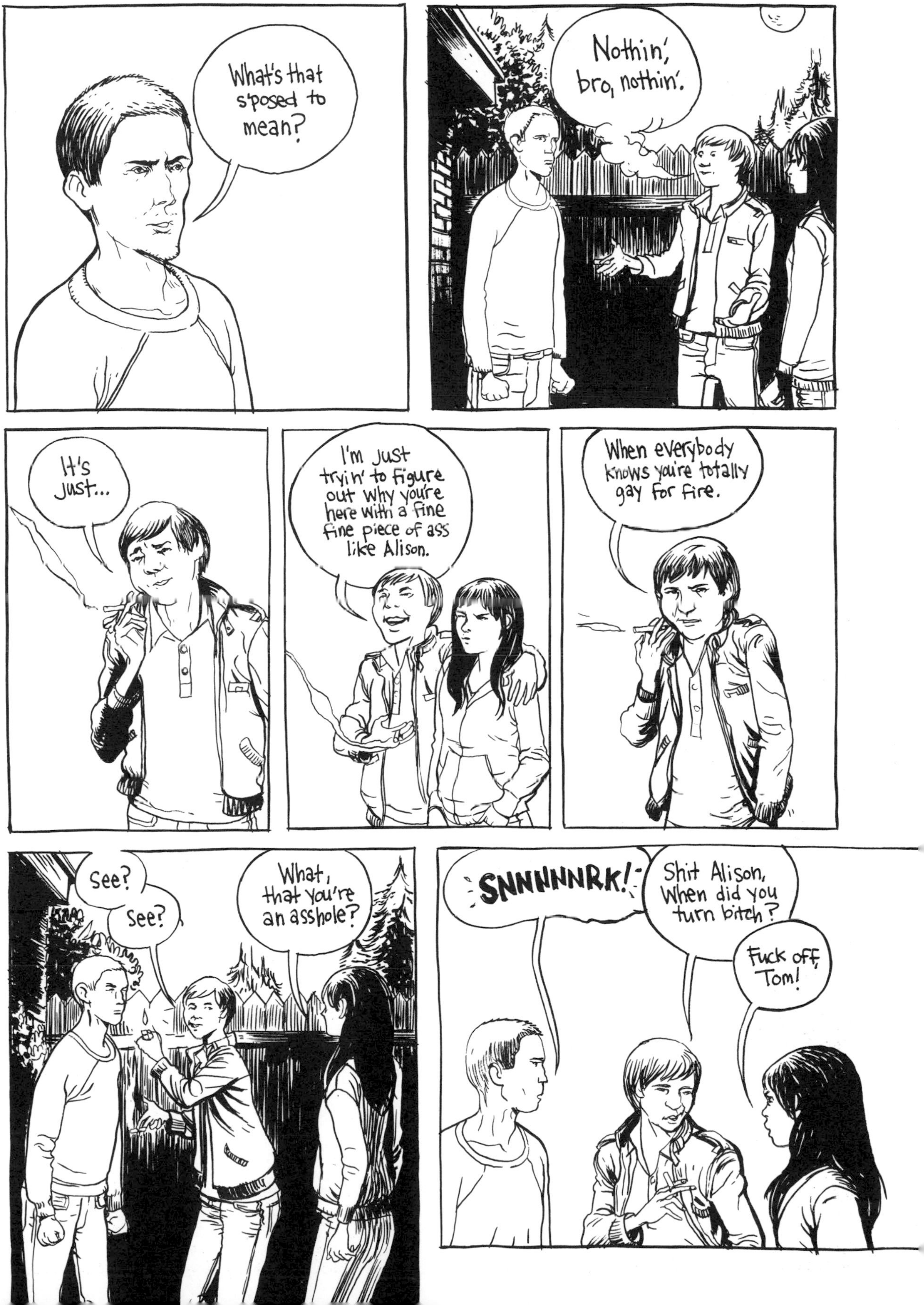
What's that s'posed to mean?
Nothin', bro, nothin'.
It's just...
I'm just tryin' to figure out why you're here with a fine fine piece of ass like Alison.
When everybody knows you're totally gay for fire.
See?
See?
What, that you're an asshole?
SNNNNNRK!
Shit Alison, When did you turn bitch?
Fuck off, Tom!

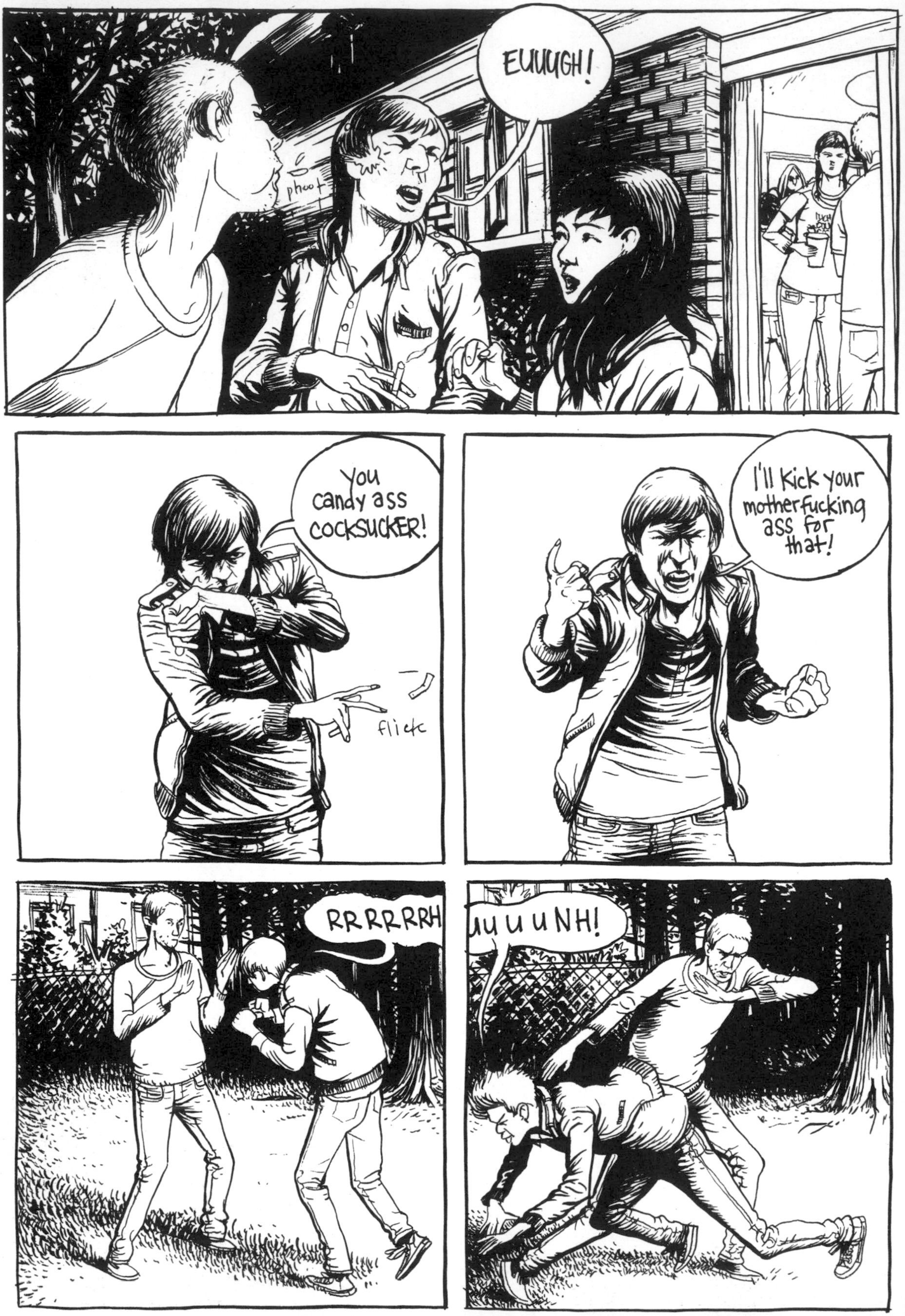
EUUUGH!
phoot
You candy ass COCKSUCKER!
flick
I'll Kick your motherfucking ass for that!
RRRRRRH
uuuuNH!

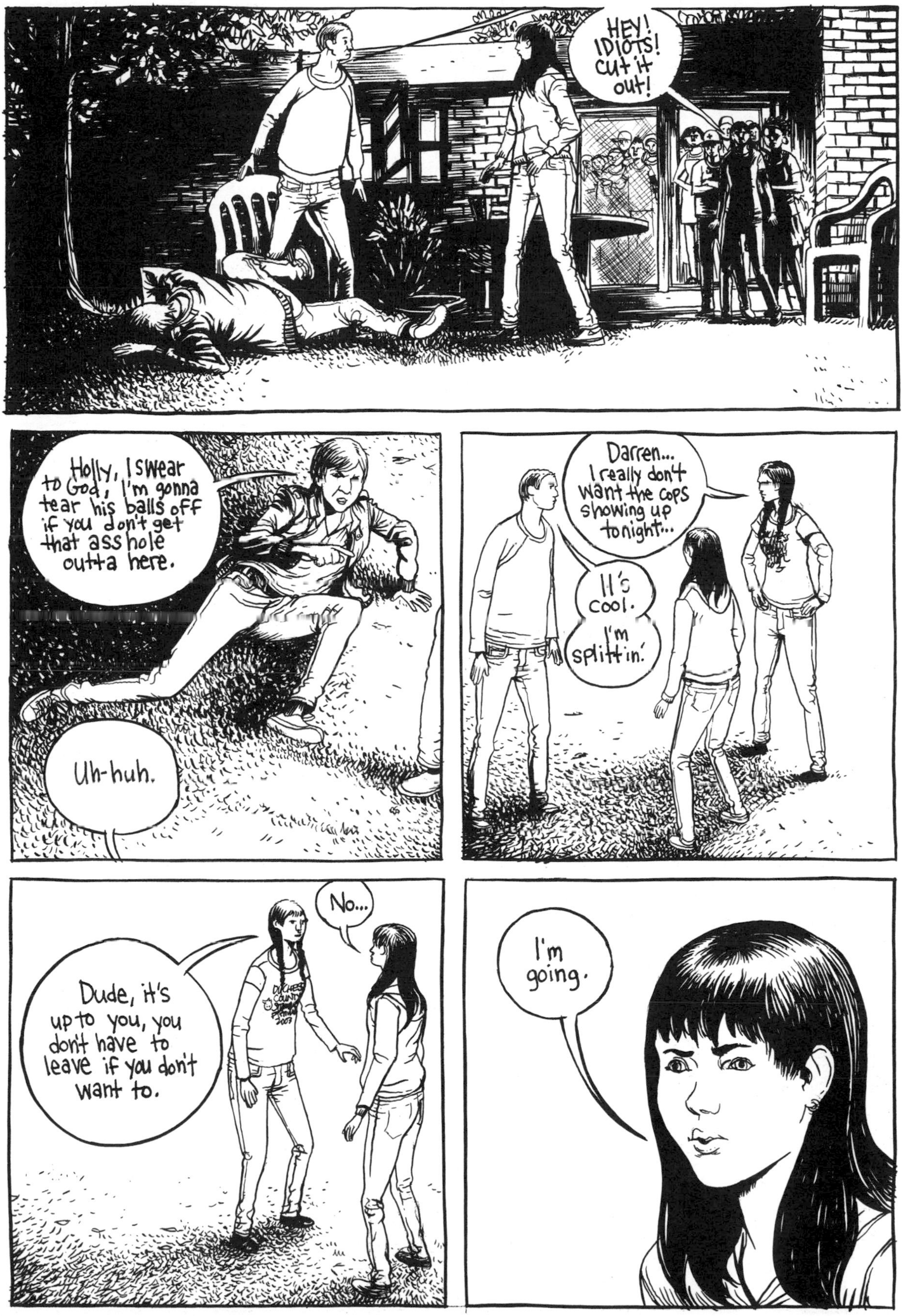
HEY! IDIOTS! CUT IT OUT!
Holly, I swear to God, I'm gonna tear his balls off if you don't get that asshole outta here.
Uh-huh.
Darren... I really don't want the cops showing up tonight...
It's cool.
I'm splittin'.
No...
Dude, it's up to you, you don't have to leave if you don't want to.
I'm going.

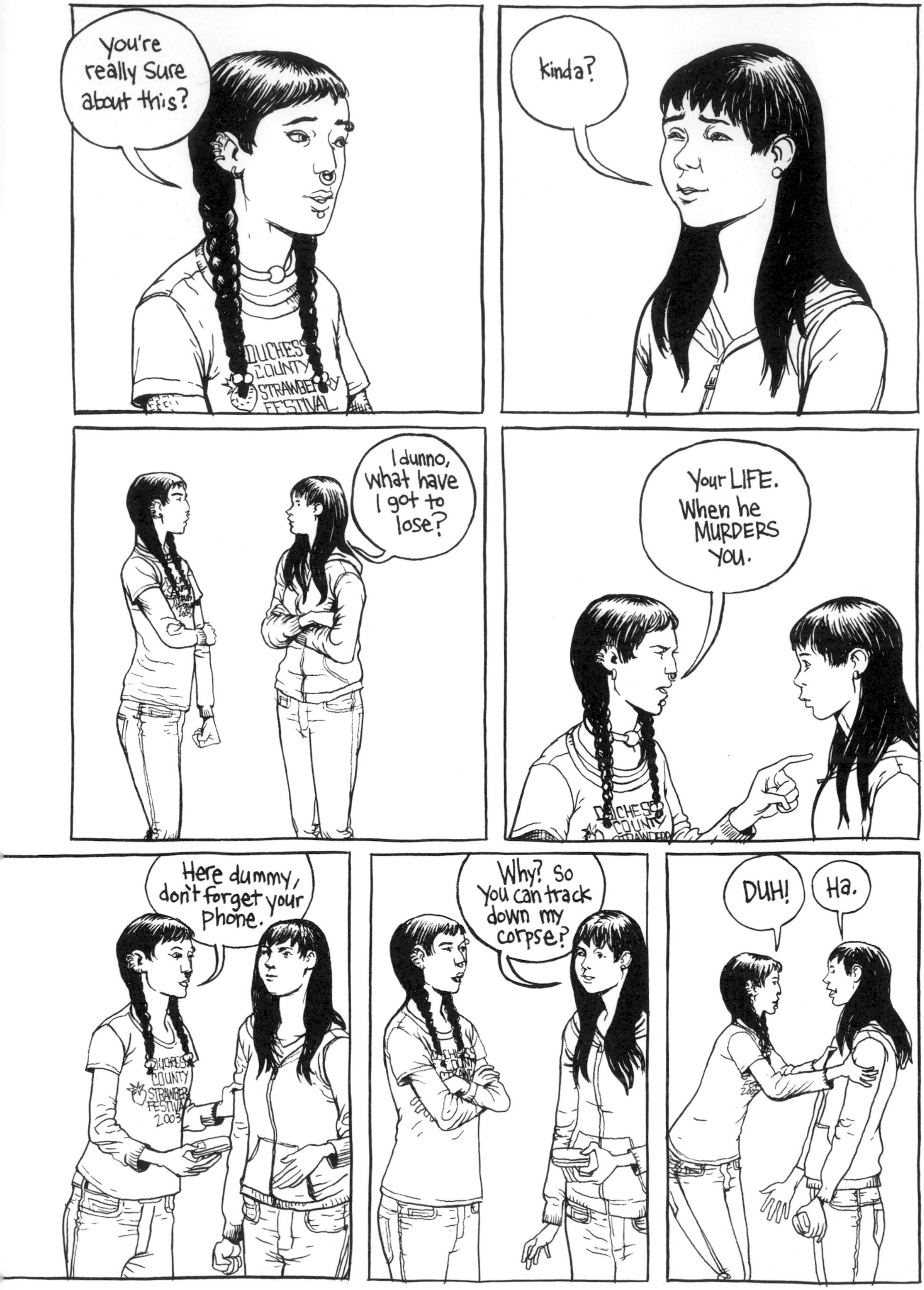
you're really Sure about this?
DUCHESS COUNTY STRAWBERRY FESTIVAL
kinda?
I dunno, what have I got to lose?
Your LIFE. When he MURDERS you.
Here dummy, don't forget your phone.
DUCHESS COUNTY STRAWBERRY FESTIVAL 2003
Why? So you can track down my corpse?
DUH!
Ha.

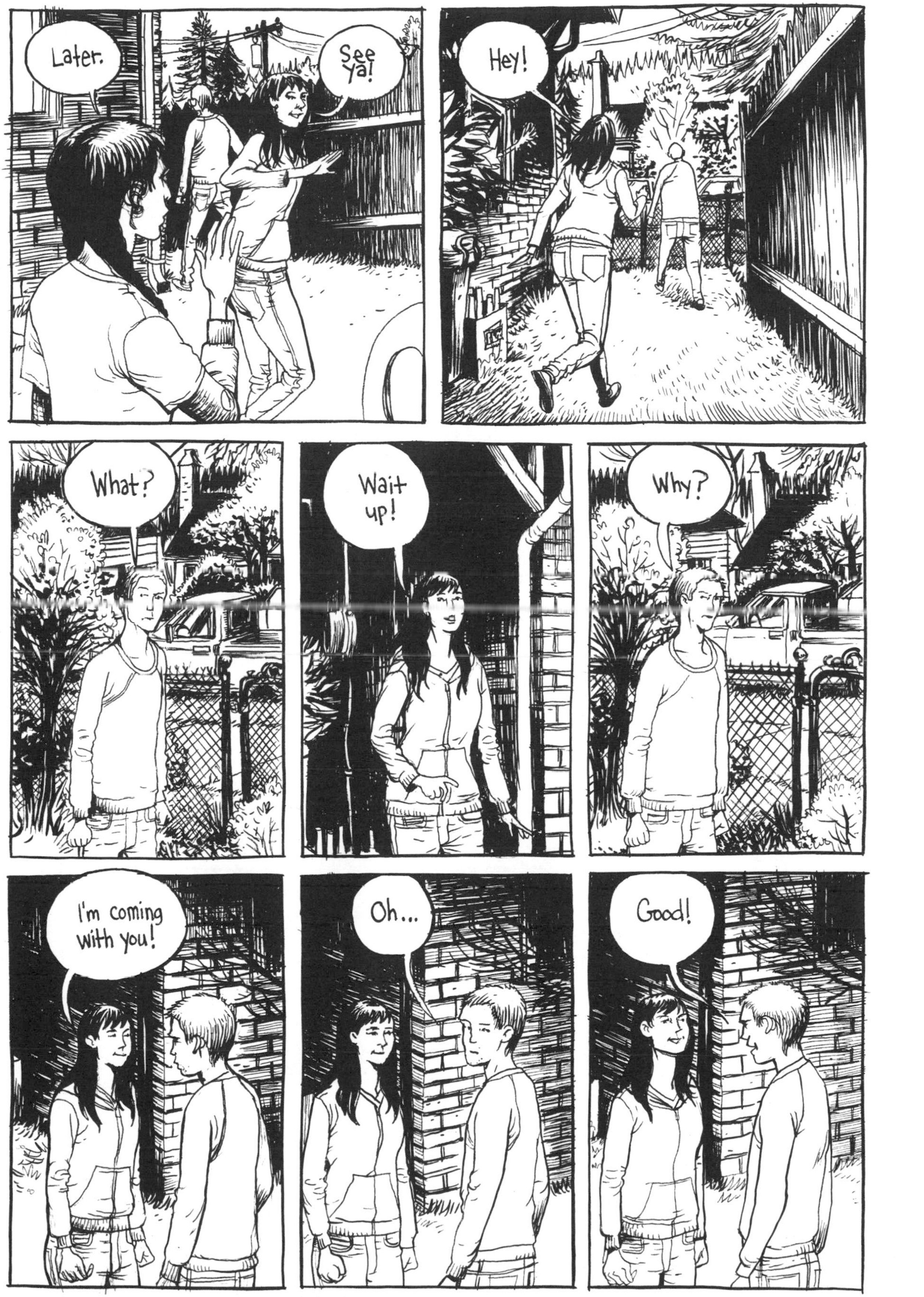
Later.
See ya!
Hey!
What?
Wait up!
Why?
I'm coming with you!
Oh...
Good!

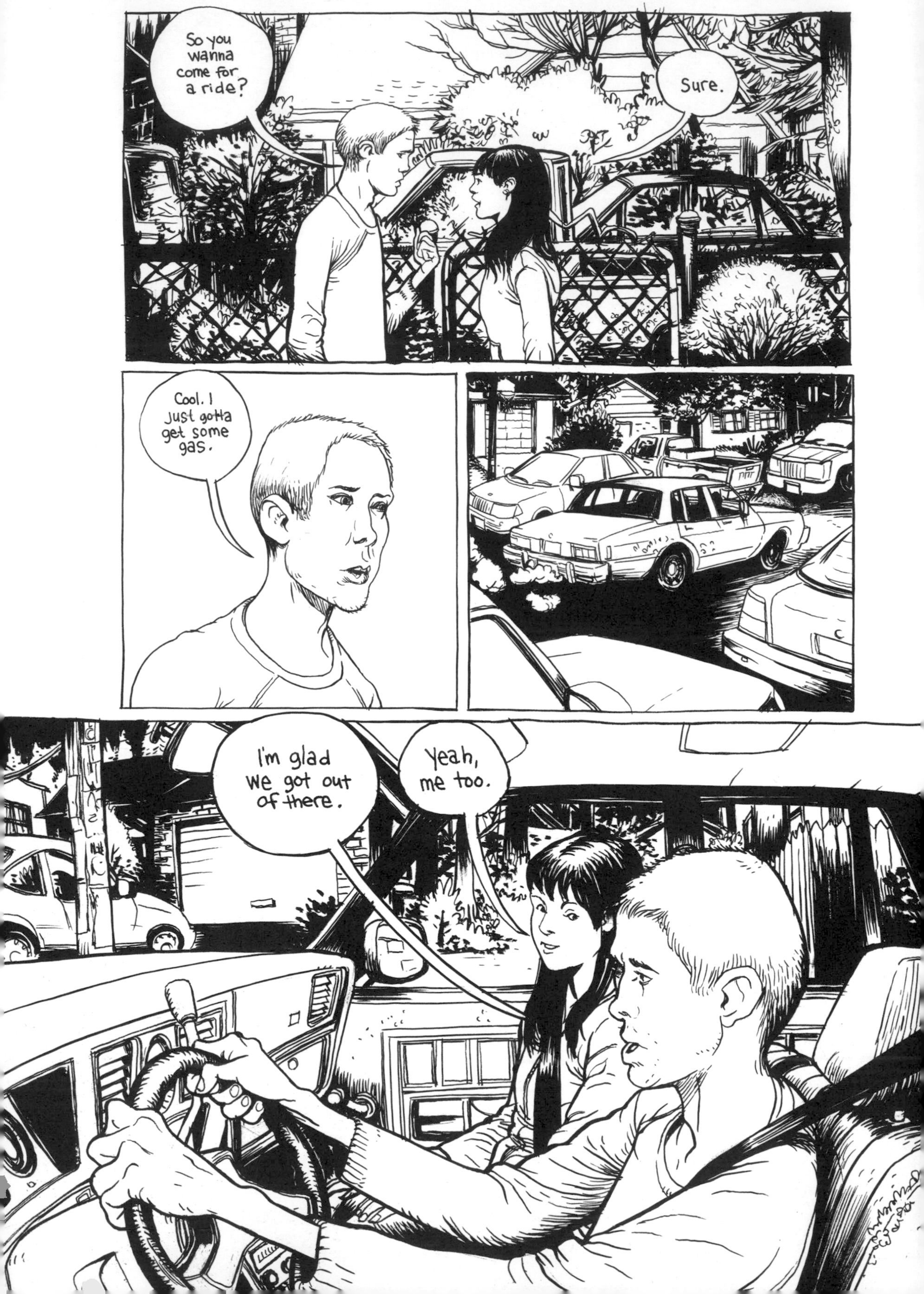
So you wanna come for a ride?
Sure.
Cool. I just gotta get some gas.
I'm glad we got out of there.
Yeah, me too.

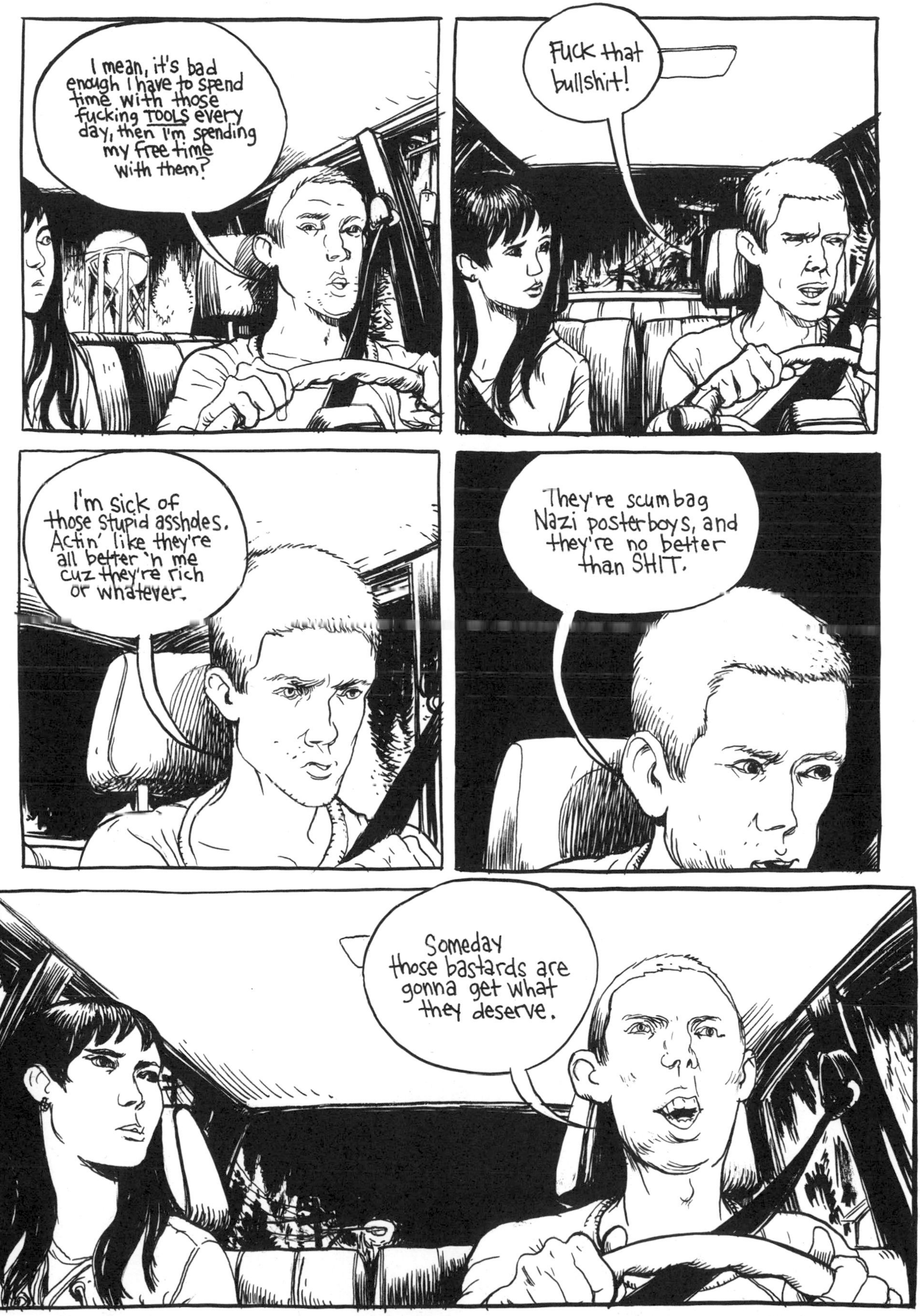
I mean, it's bad enough I have to spend time with those fucking TOOLS every day, then I'm spending my free time with them?
Fuck that bullshit!
I'm sick of those stupid assholes. Actin' like they're all better 'n me cuz they're rich or whatever.
They're scumbag Nazi posterboys, and they're no better than SHIT.
Someday those bastards are gonna get what they deserve.

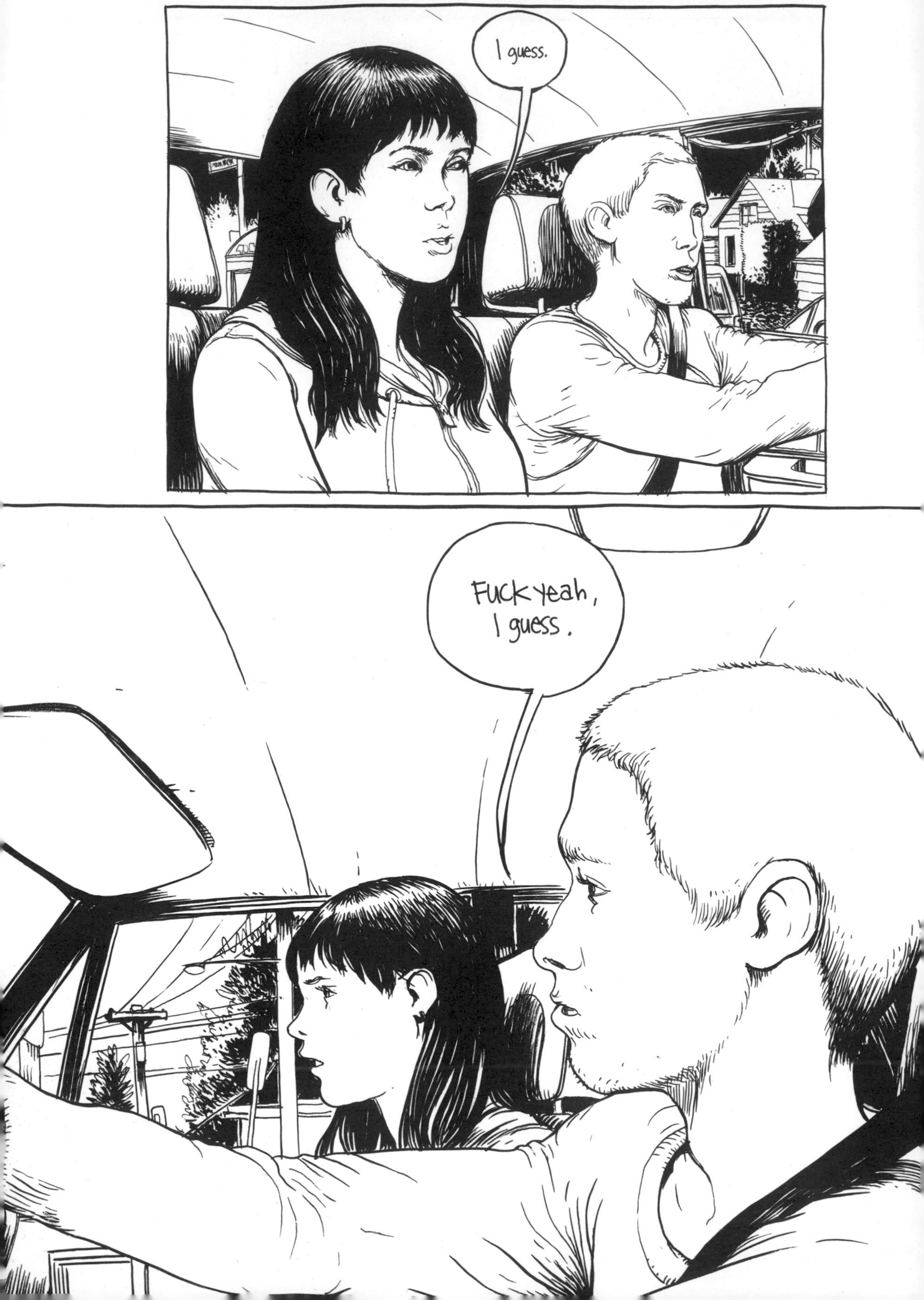
I guess.
Fuck yeah, I guess.

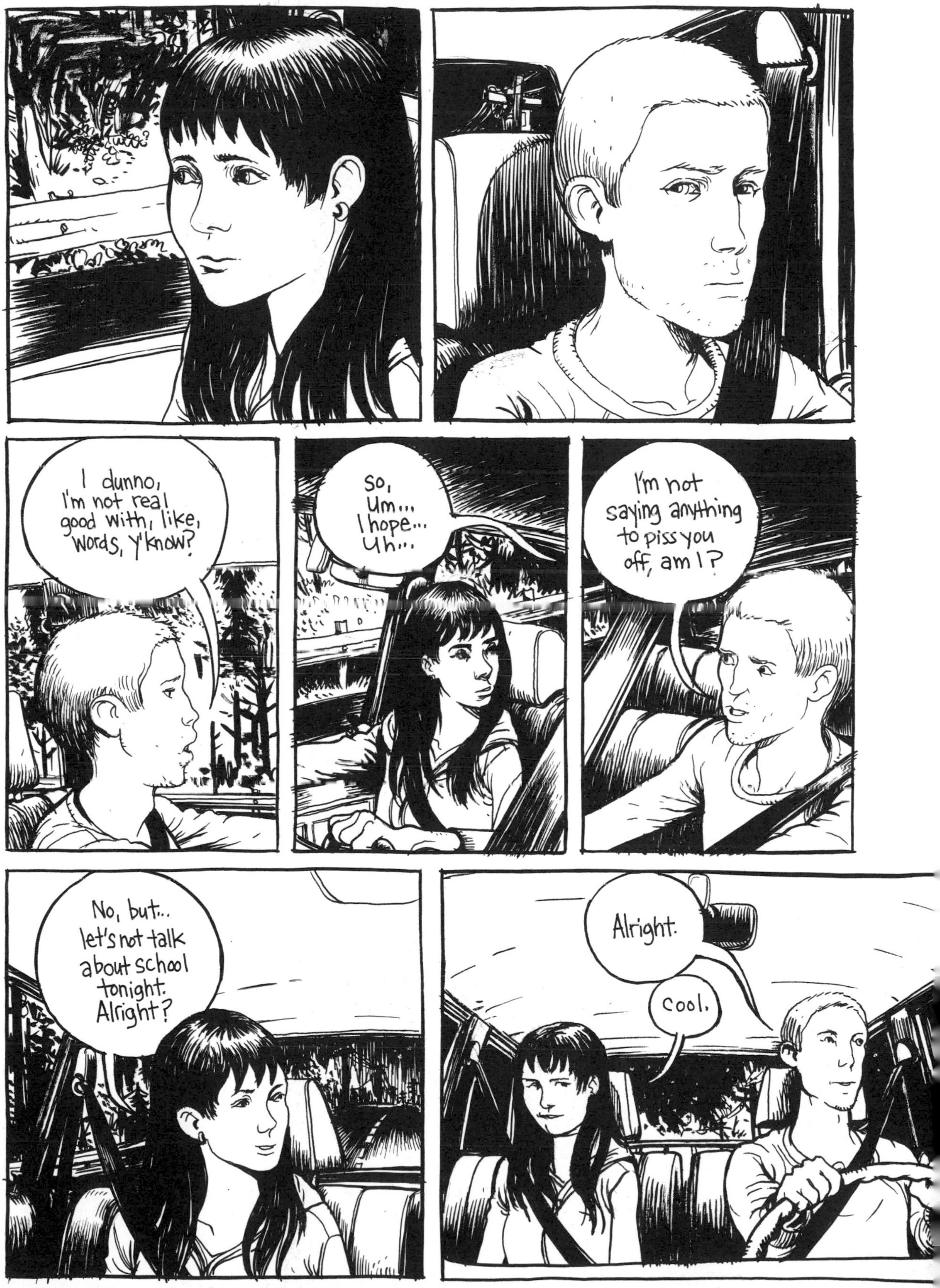
I dunno, I'm not real good with, like, words, y'know?
So, um... I hope... uh...
I'm not saying anything to piss you off, am I?
No, but... let's not talk about school tonight. Alright?
Alright.
Cool.

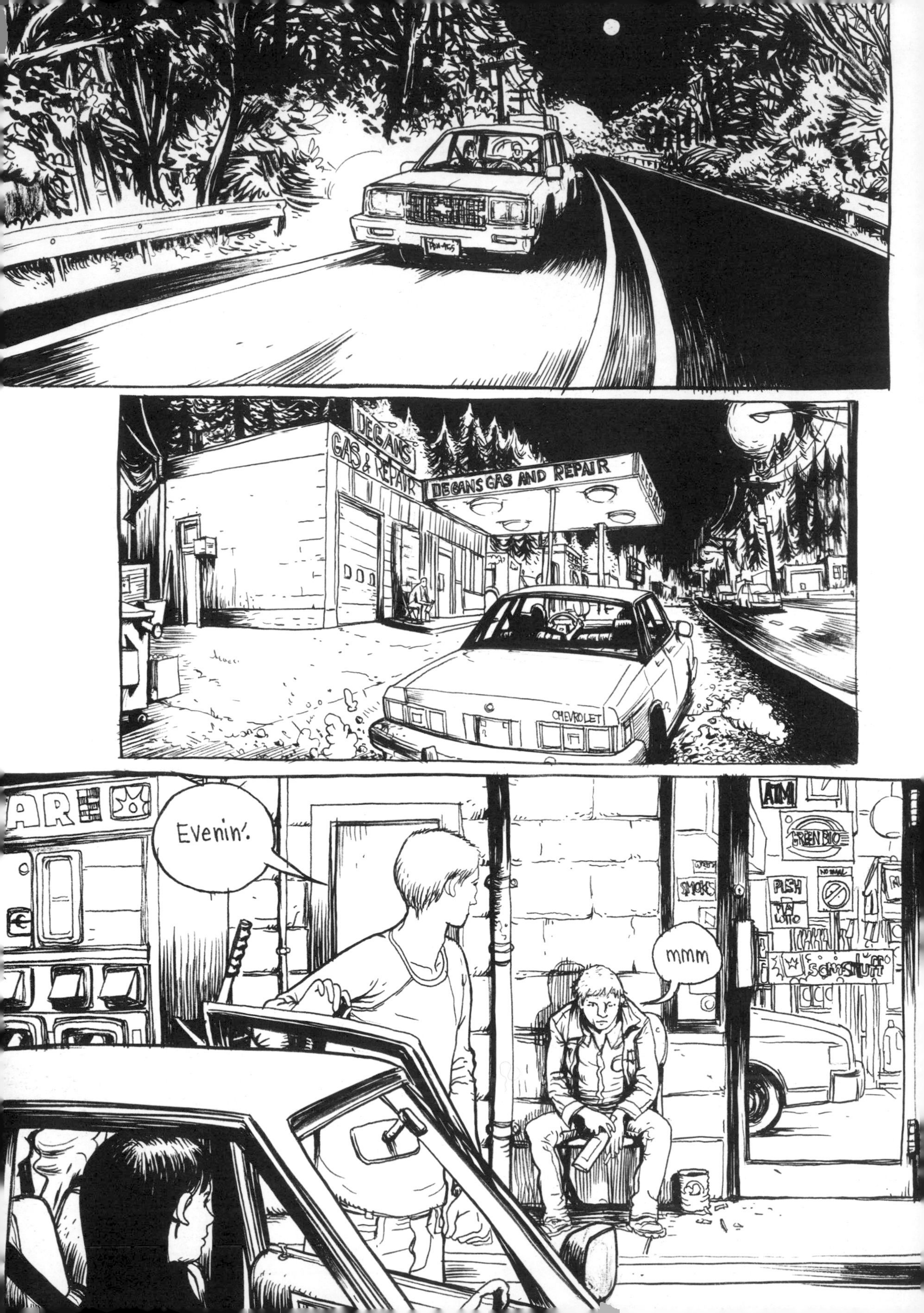
DEGANS
GAS & REPAIR
DEGANS GAS AND REPAIR
DEGANS
CHEVROLET
Evenin'.
mmm
ATM
GREEN BIO
SMOKES
PUSH
PLAY LOTTO
samstuff

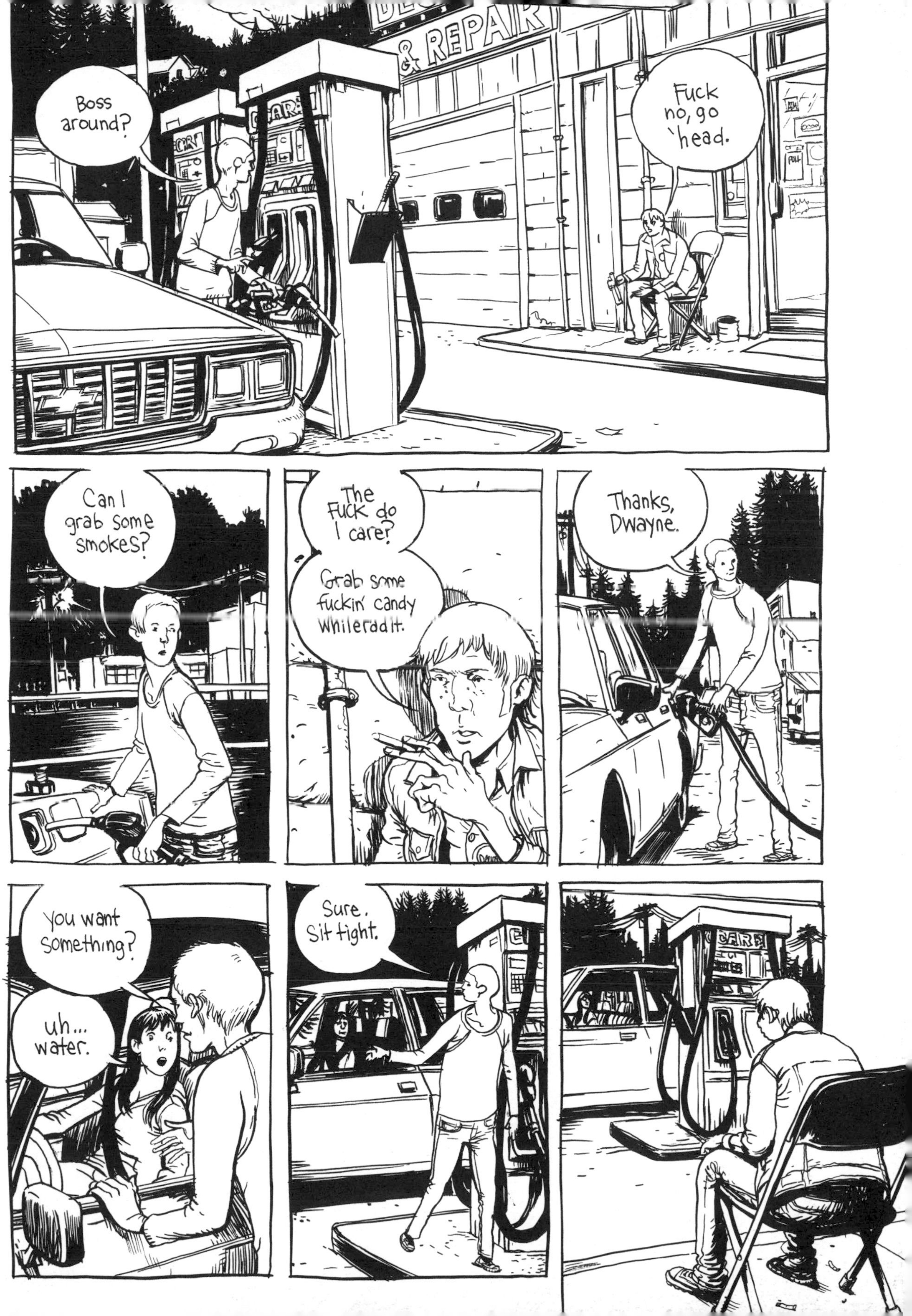
& REPAIR
Boss around?
Fuck no, go `head.
Can I grab some smokes?
The Fuck do I care?
Grab some fuckin' candy whileradit.
Thanks, Dwayne.
you want something?
uh... water.
Sure. Sit tight.

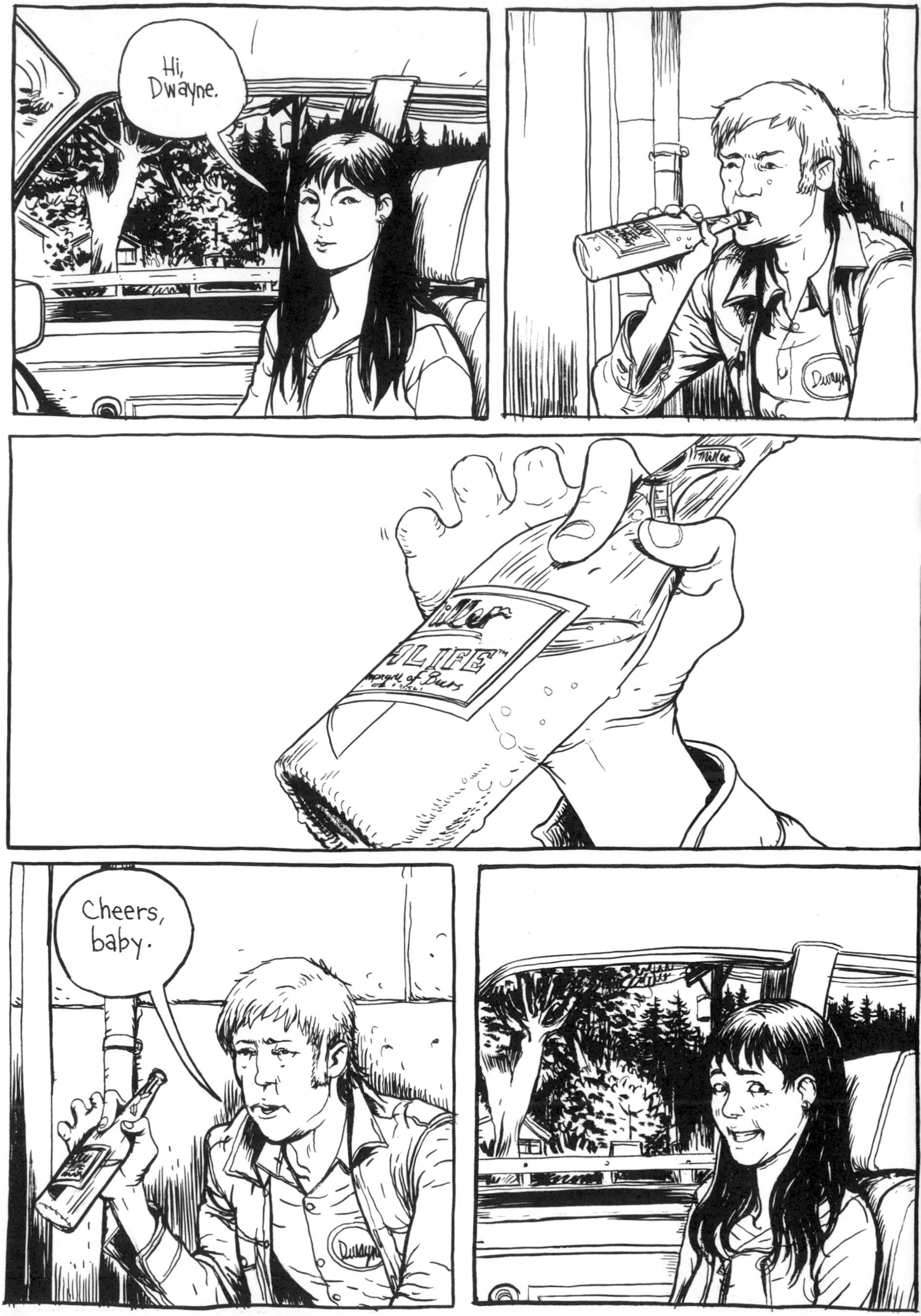
Hi, Dwayne.
Cheers, baby.

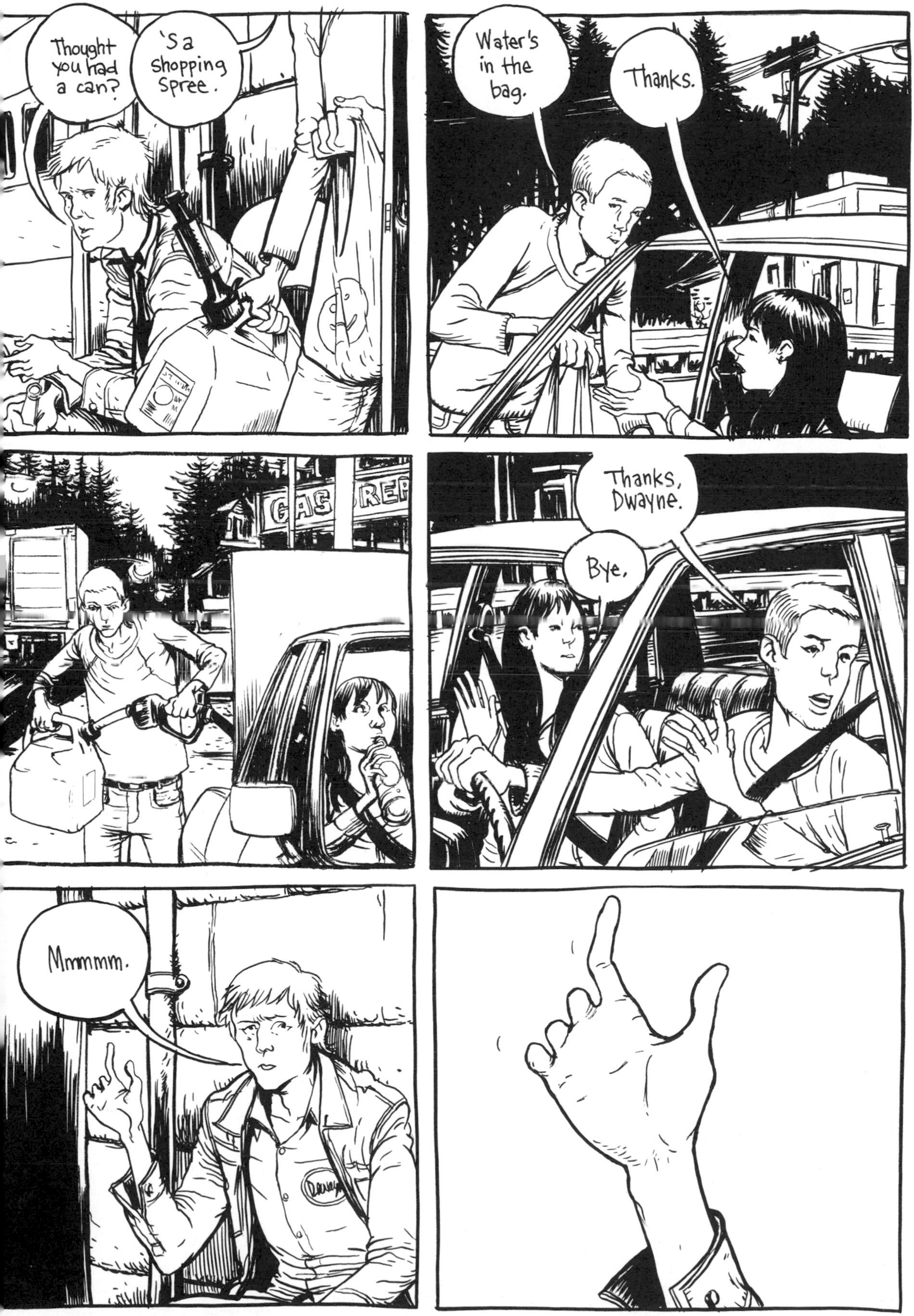
Thought you had a can?
'S a shopping spree.
Water's in the bag.
Thanks.
Thanks, Dwayne.
Bye.
Mmmmm.

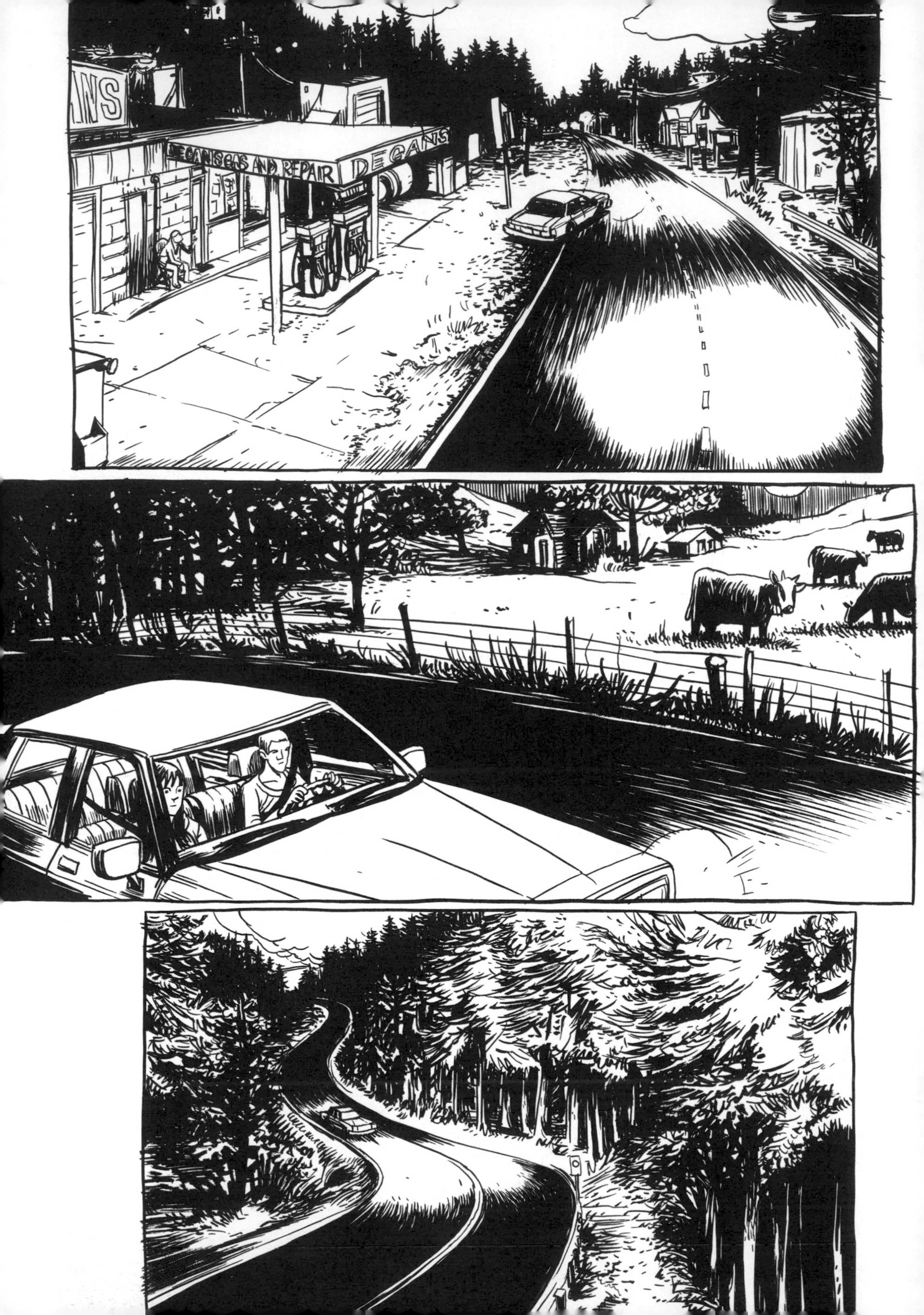
ANS
DEGANS GAS AND REPAIR
DEGANS

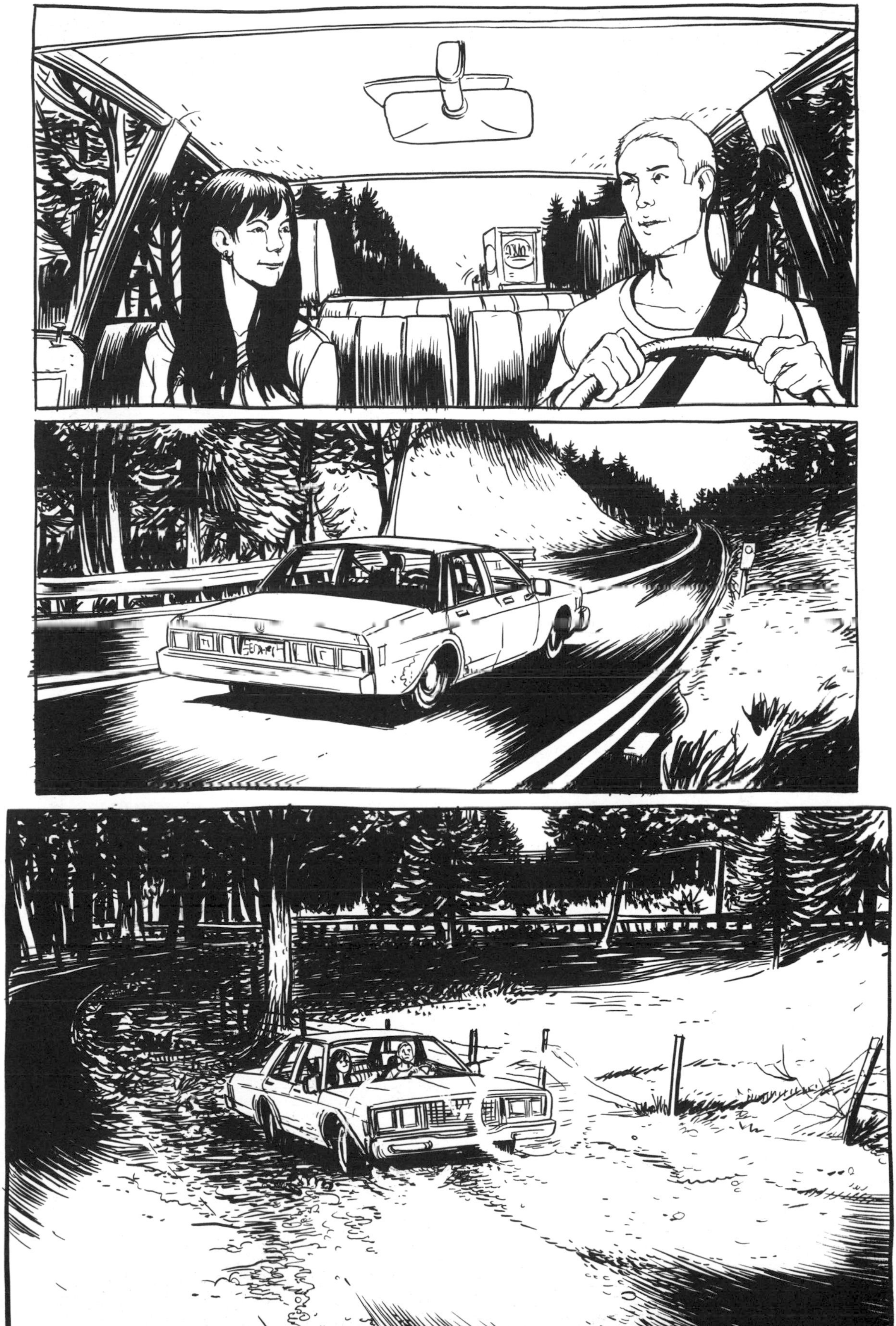

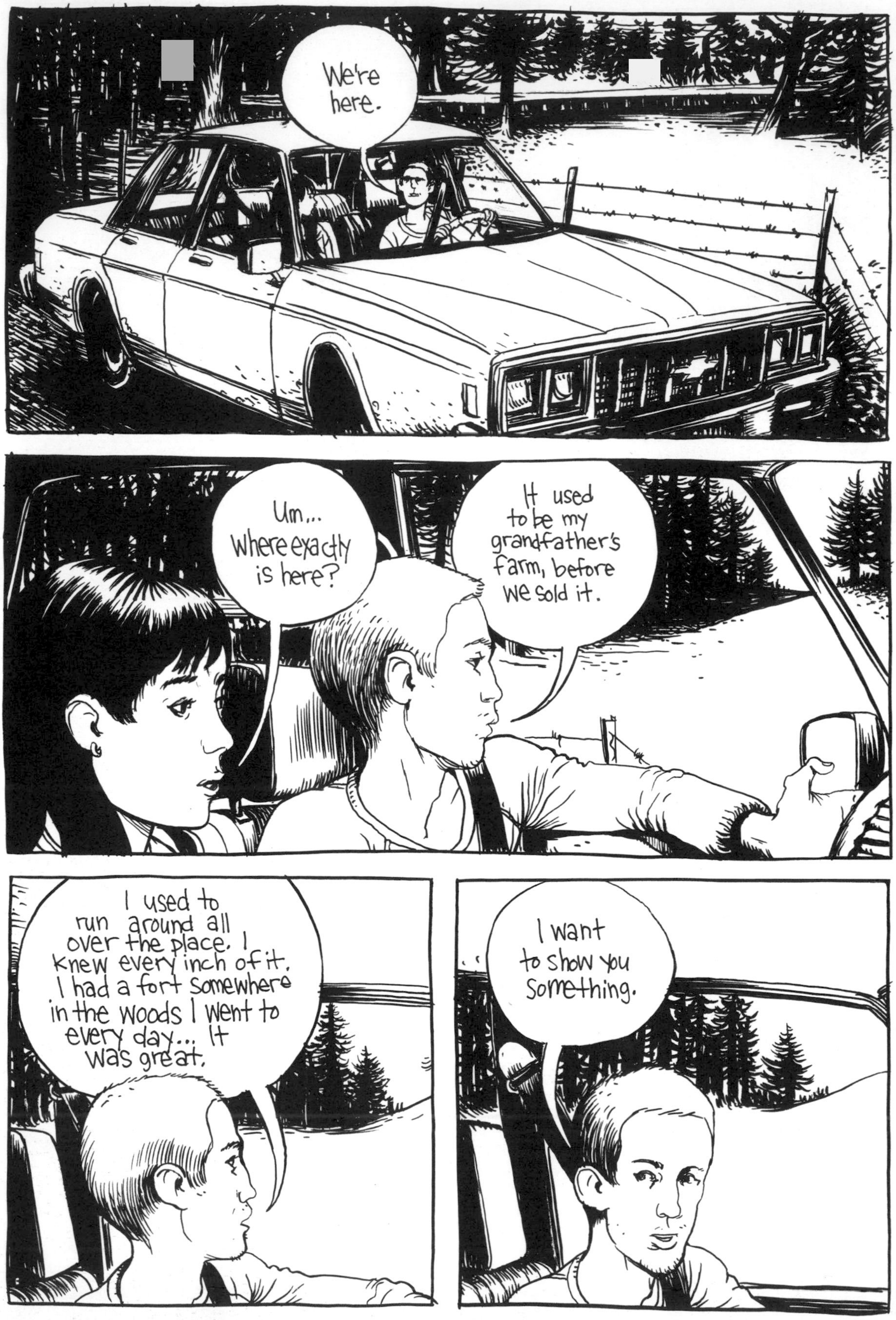
We're here.
Um... Where exactly is here?
It used to be my grandfather's farm, before we sold it.
I used to run around all over the place. I knew every inch of it. I had a fort somewhere in the woods I went to every day... It was great.
I want to show you something.

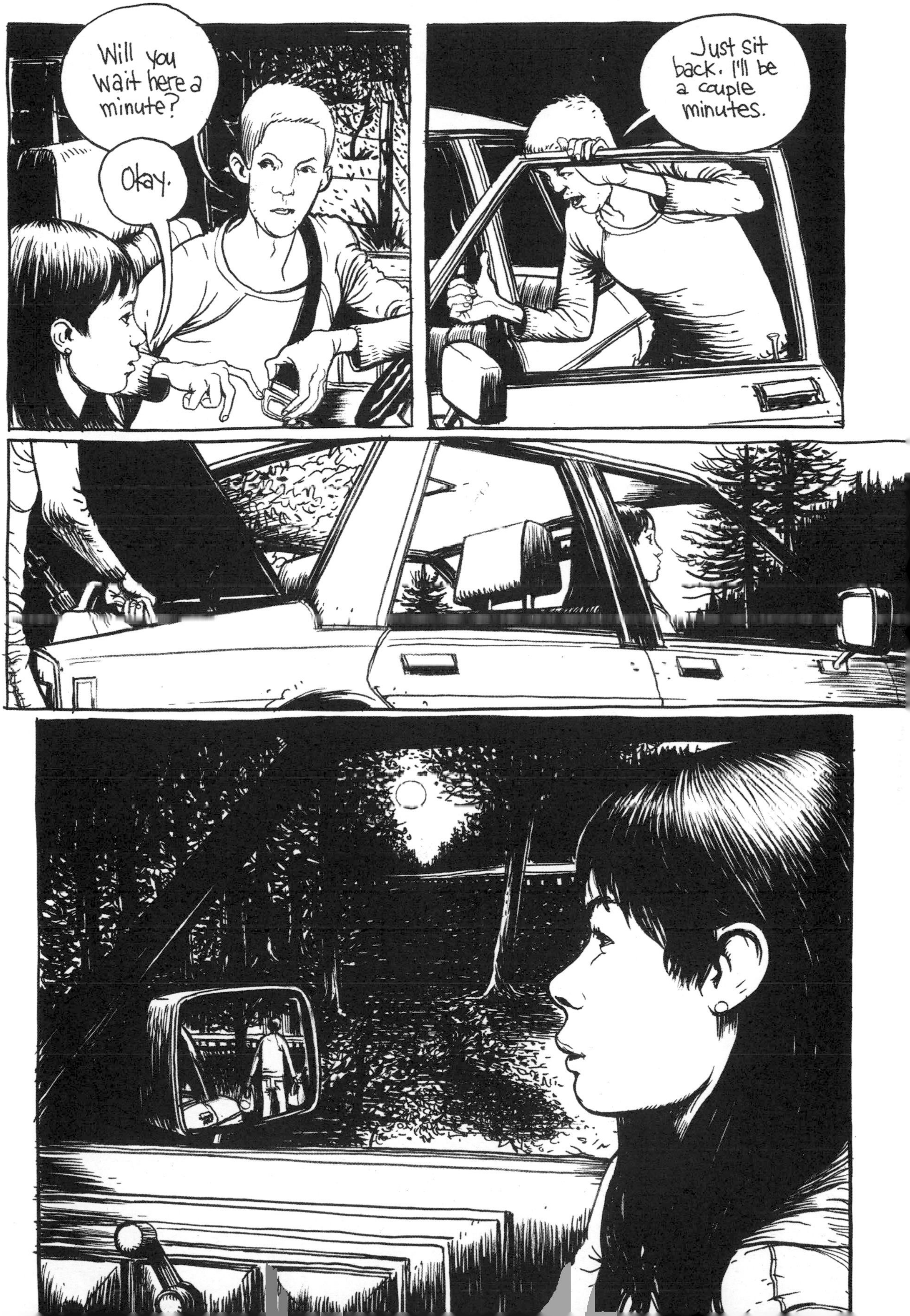
Will you wait here a minute?
Okay.
Just sit back. I'll be a couple minutes.

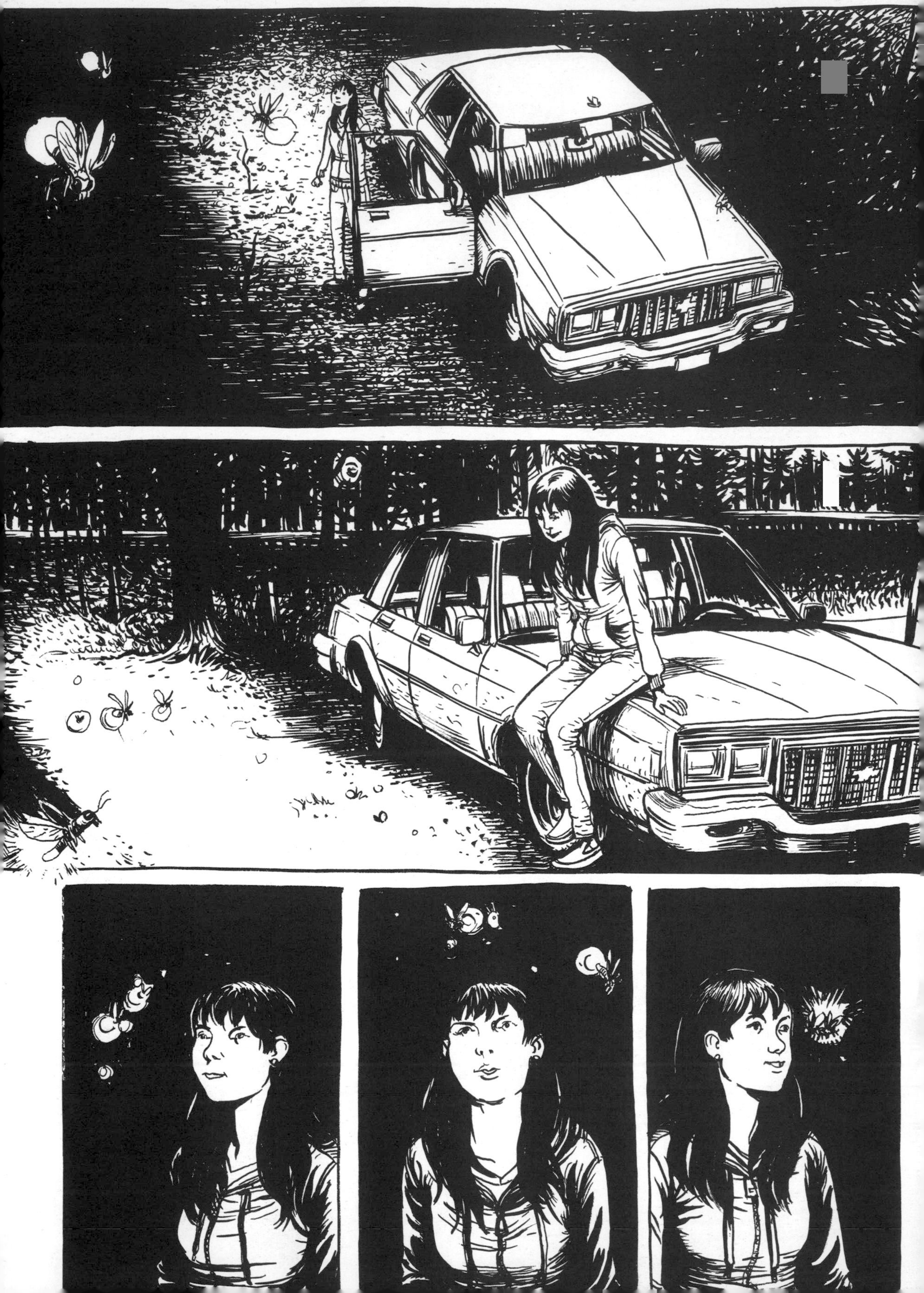

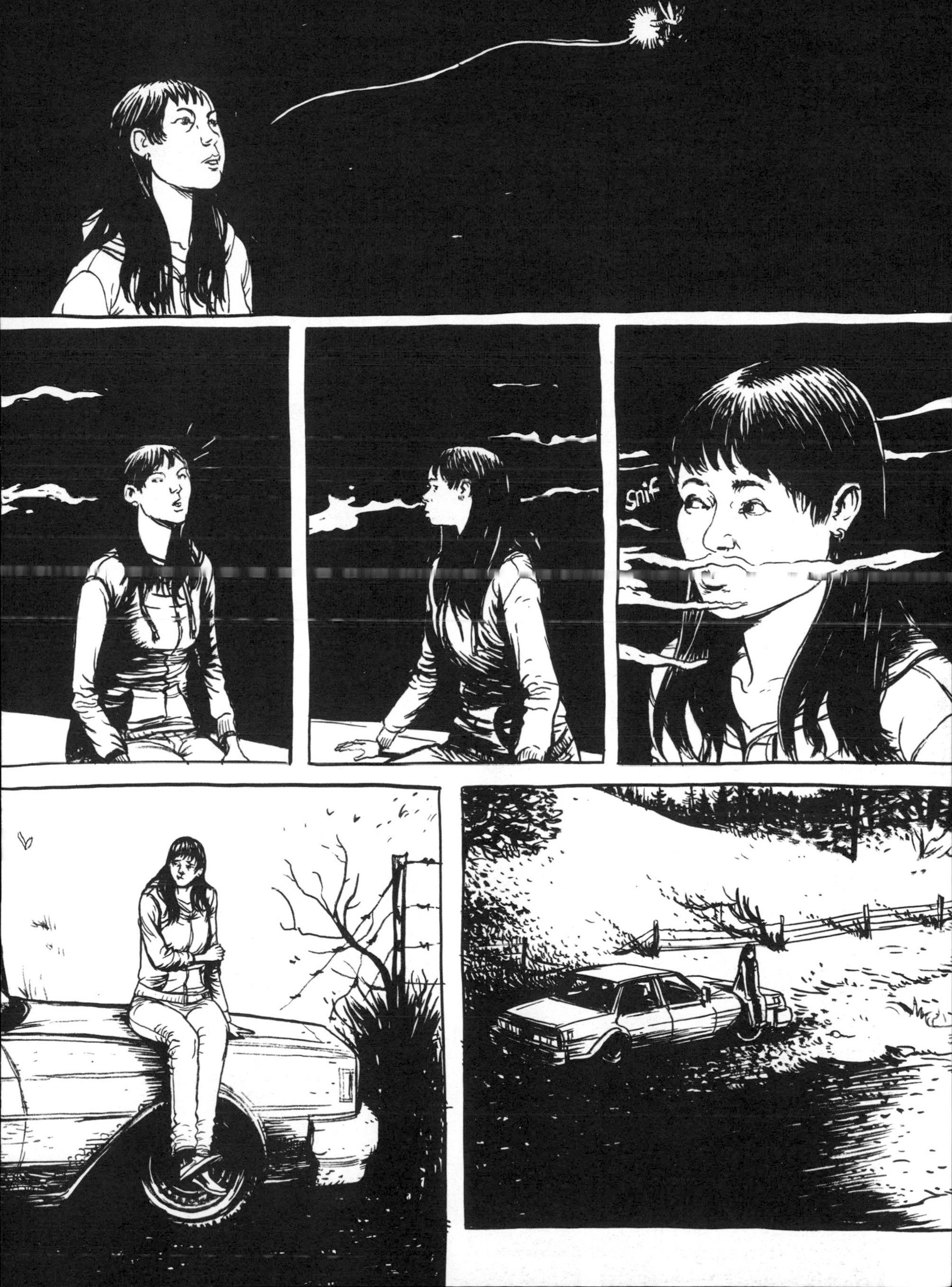
snif

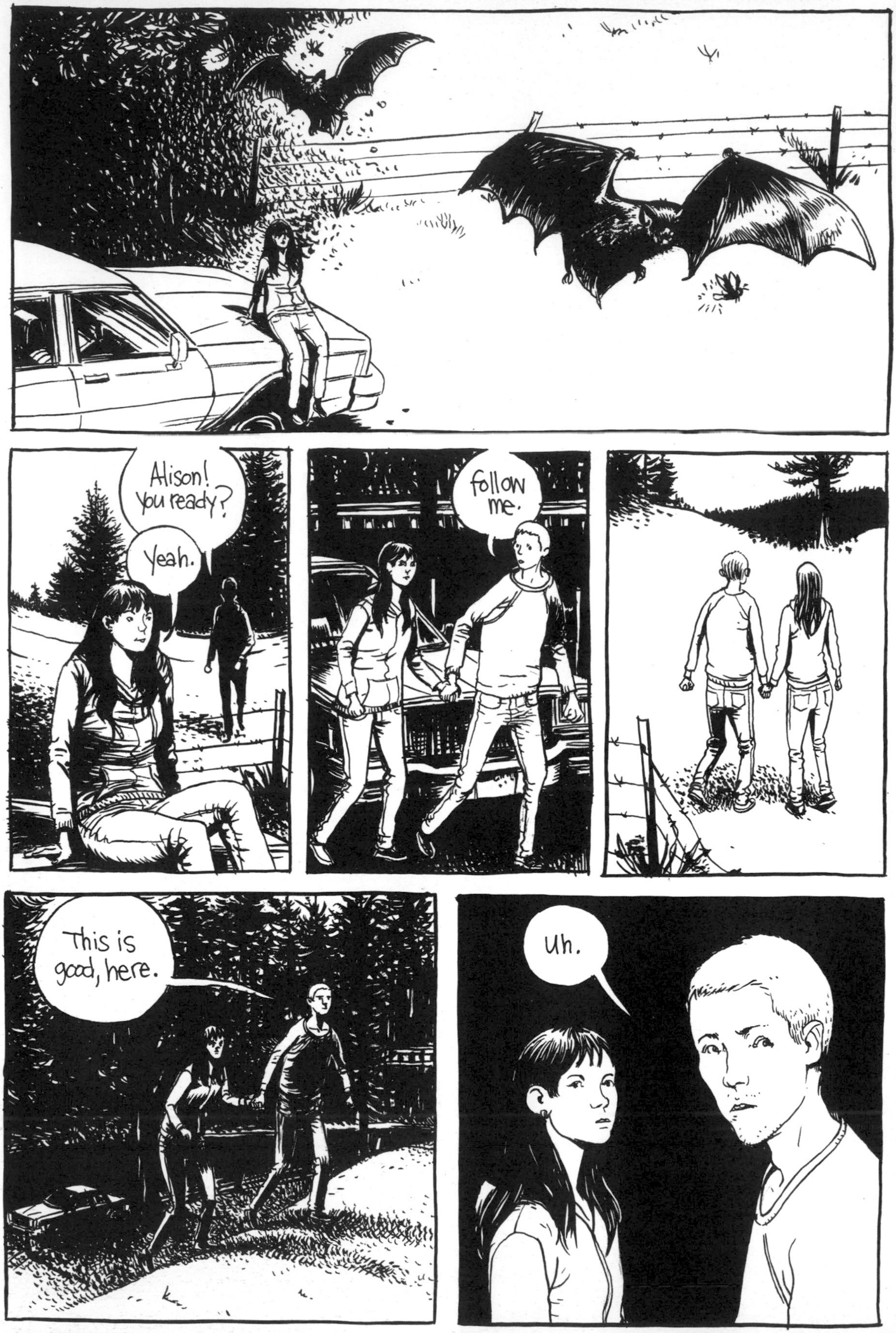
Alison! you ready?
Yeah.
follow me.
This is good, here.
Uh.

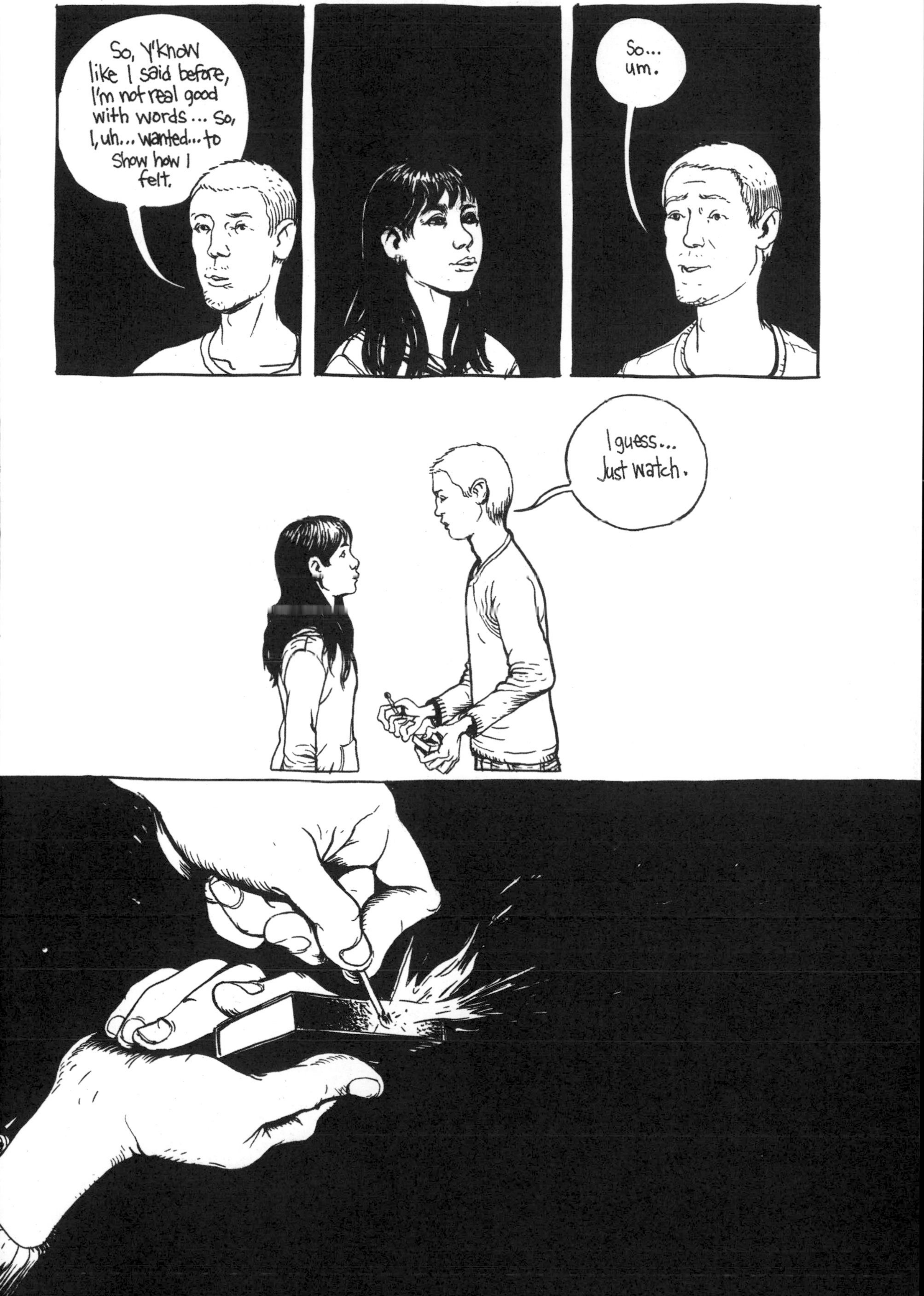
So, Y'know like I said before, I'm not real good with words... So, I, uh... wanted... to show how I felt.
So... um.
I guess... Just watch.

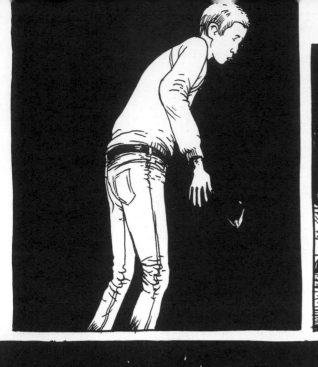

FWOOMP!

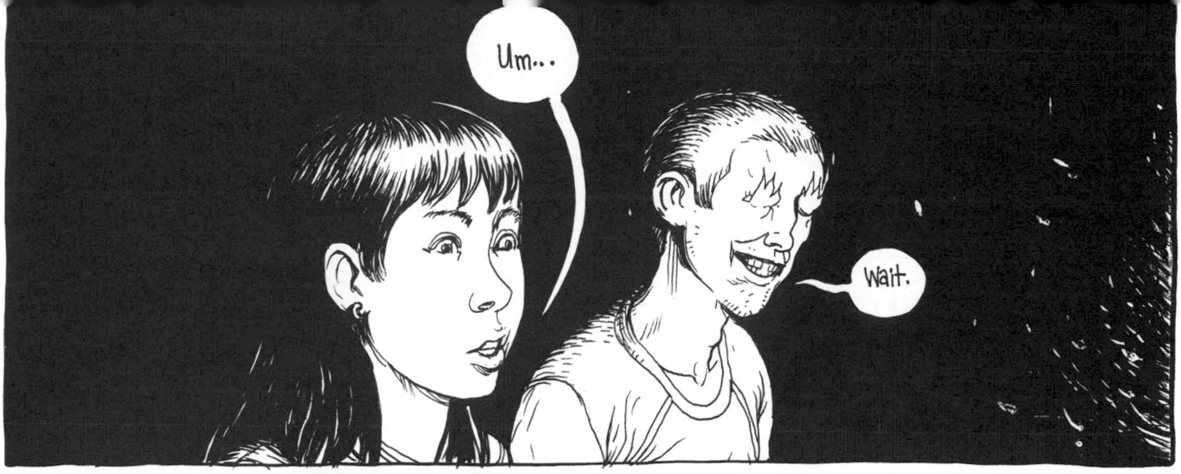
Um...
Wait.

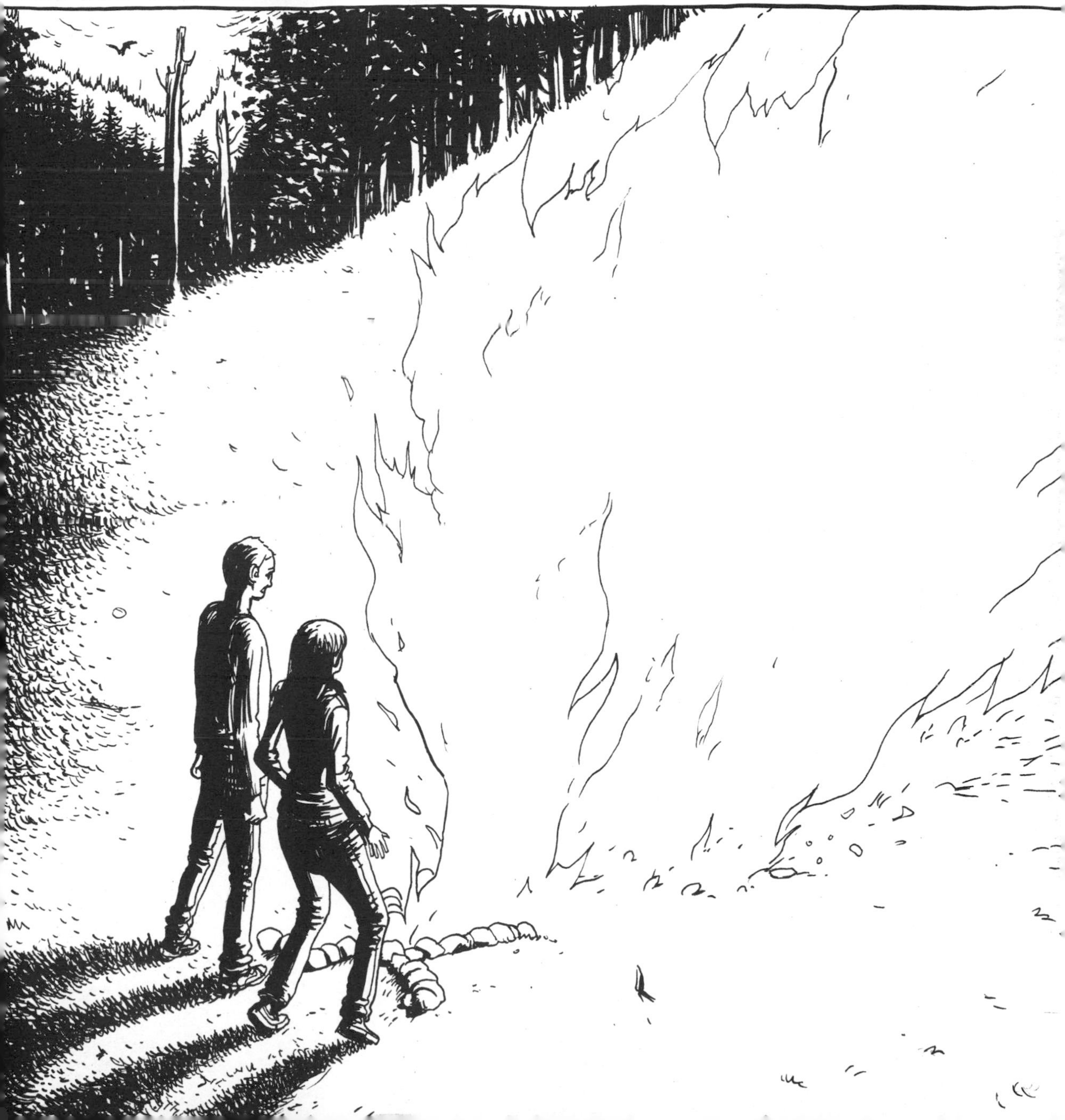

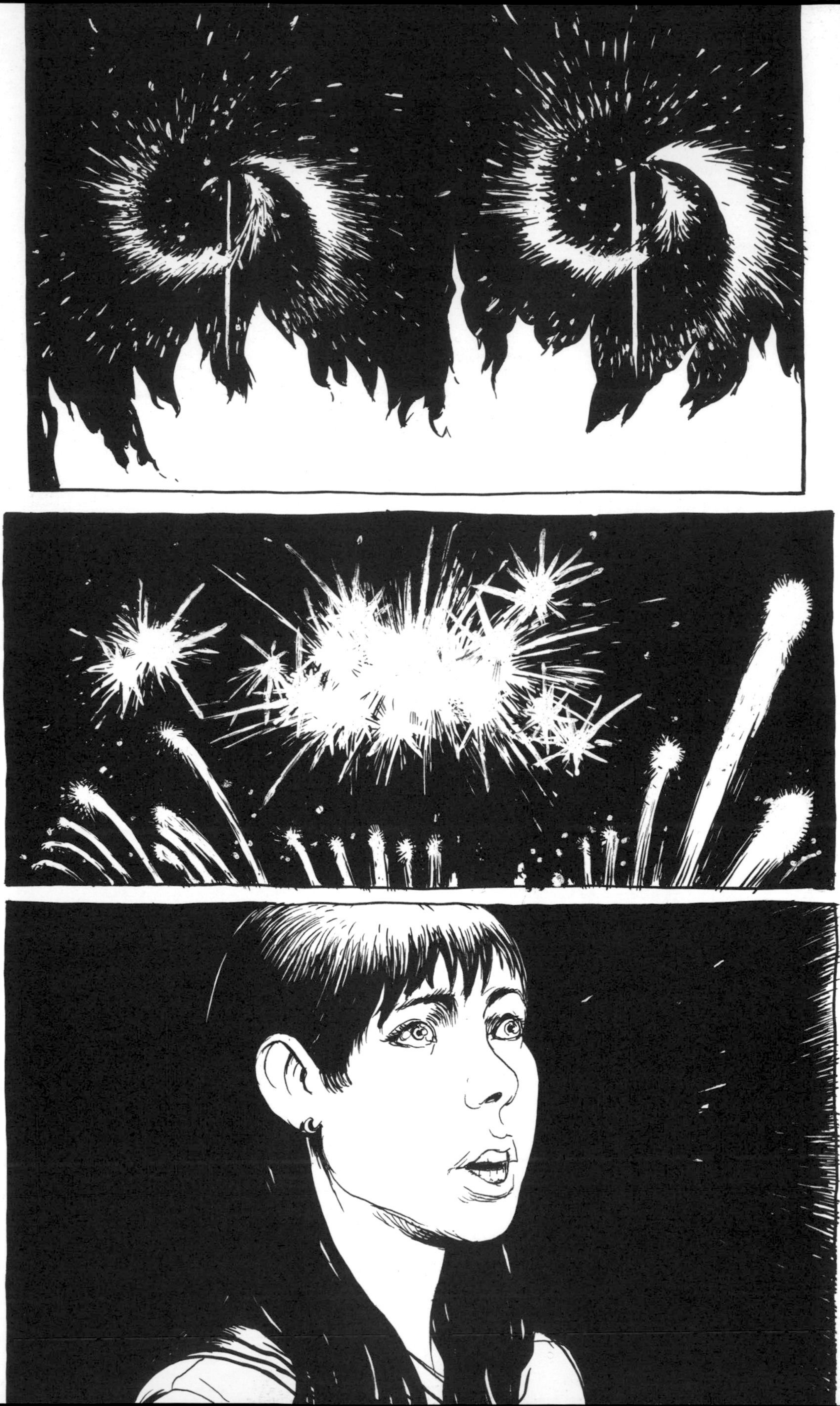

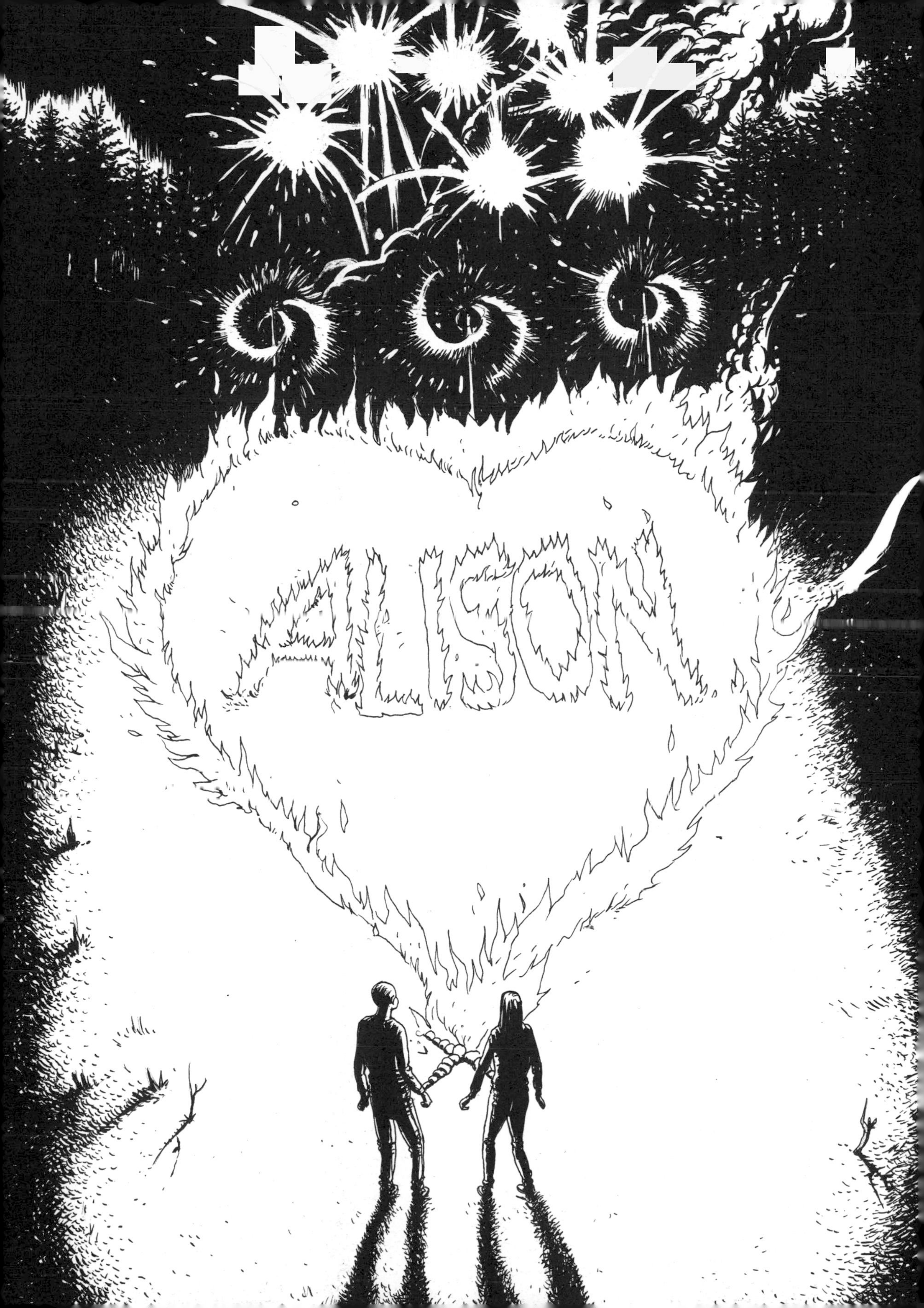
ALISON

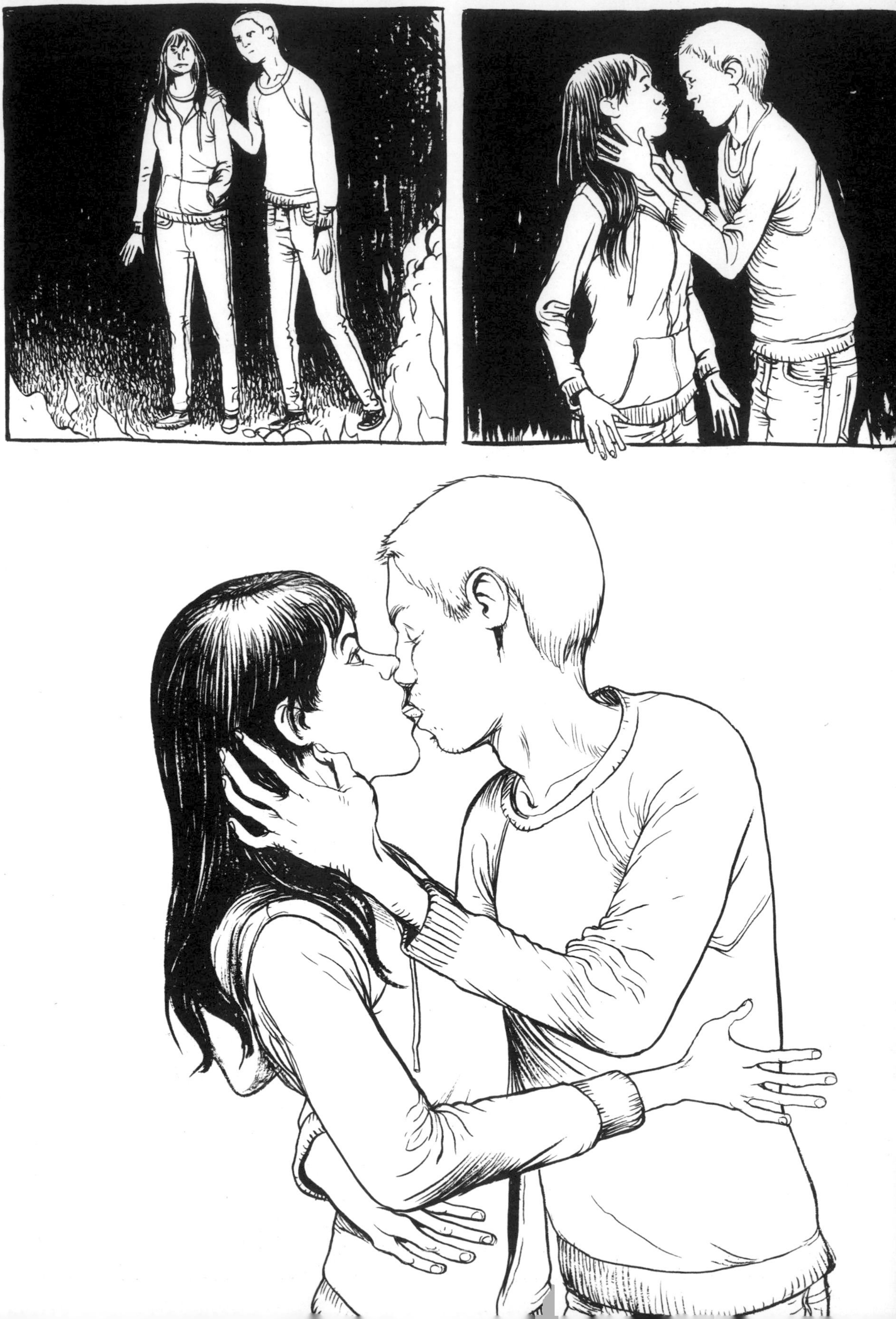

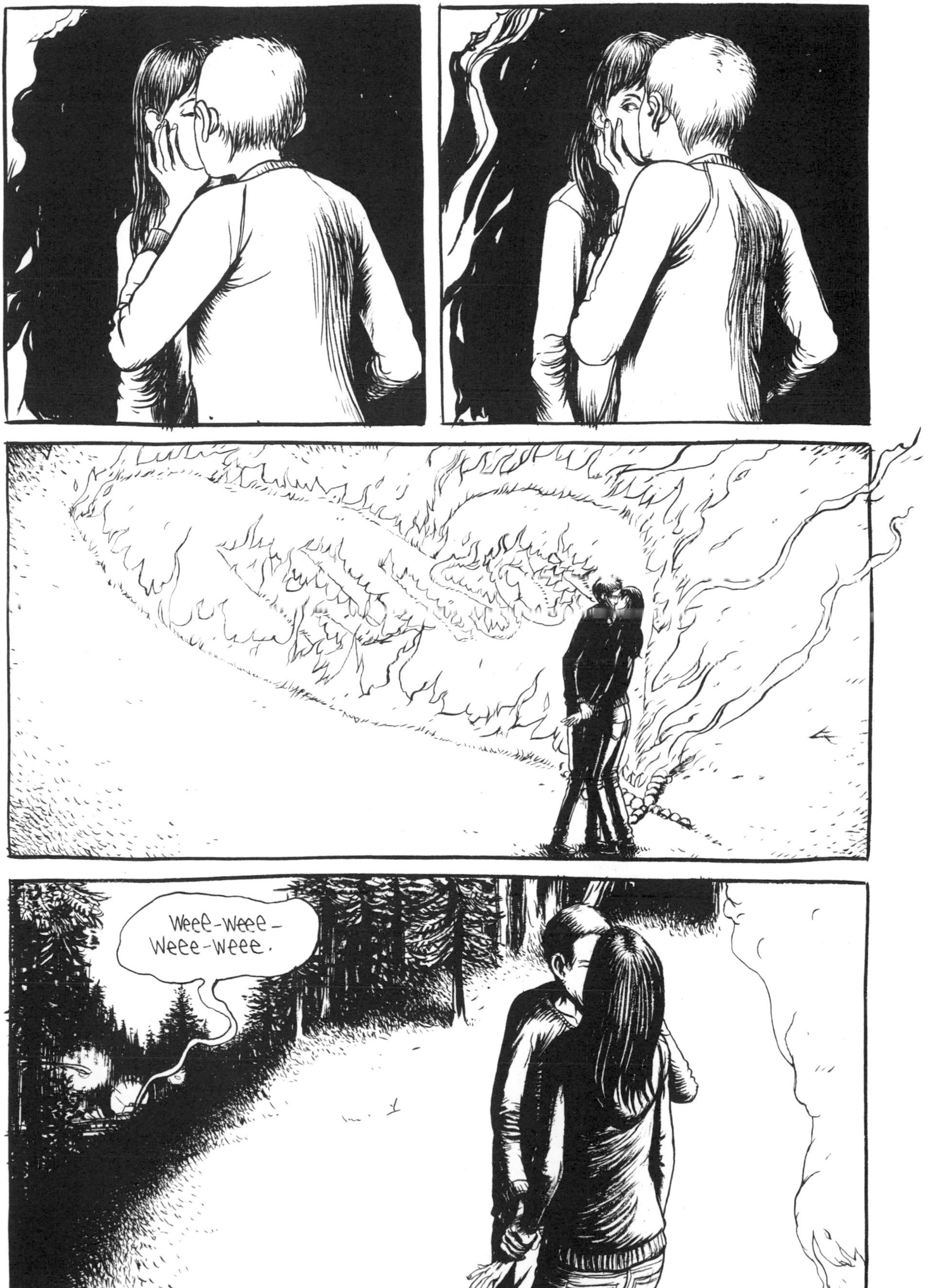
Weee-weee-
Weee-weee.

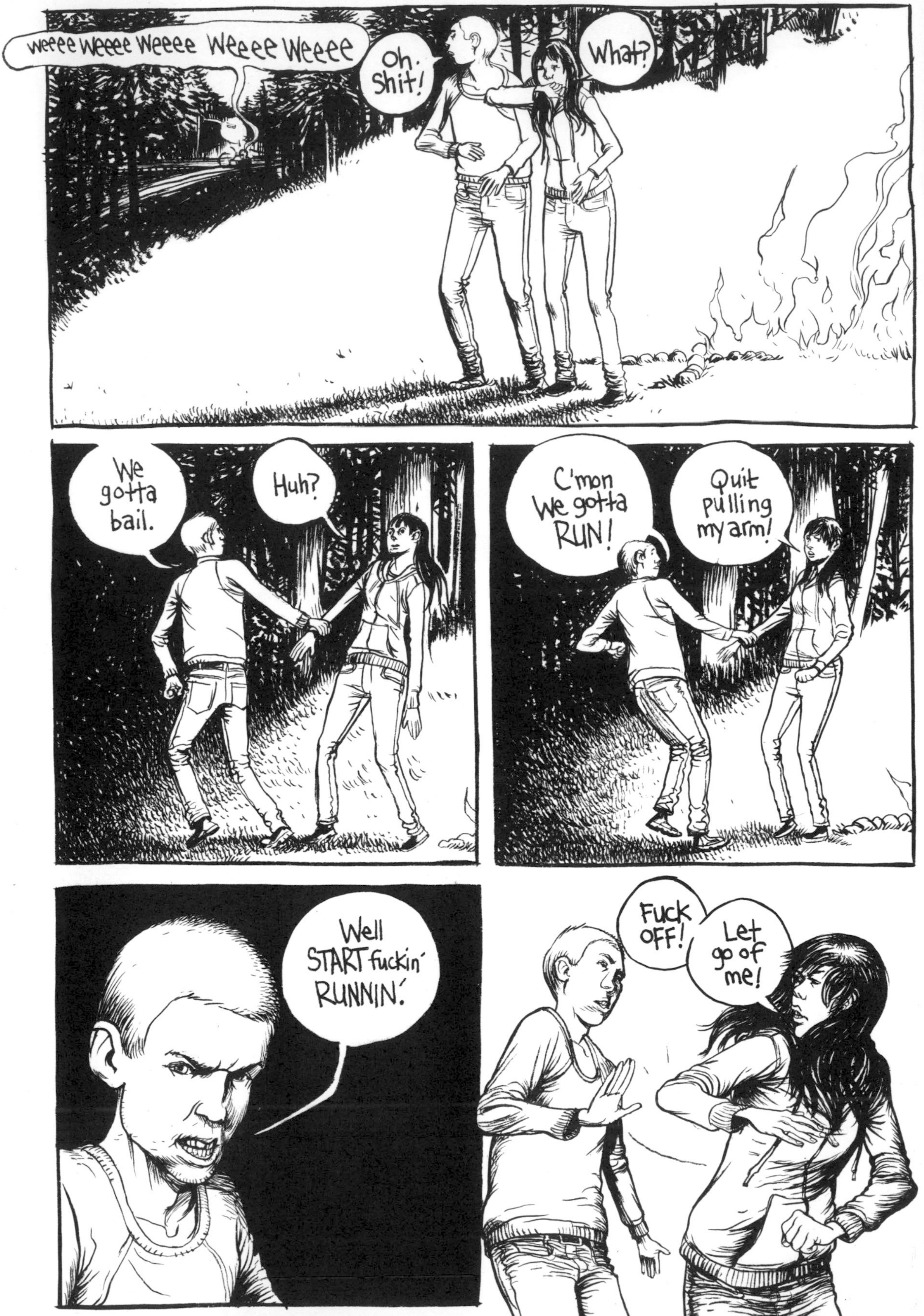
weeee weeee weeee weeee weeee
Oh. Shit!
What?
We gotta bail.
Huh?
C'mon We gotta RUN!
Quit pulling my arm!
Well START fuckin' RUNNIN'.
FUCK OFF!
Let go of me!

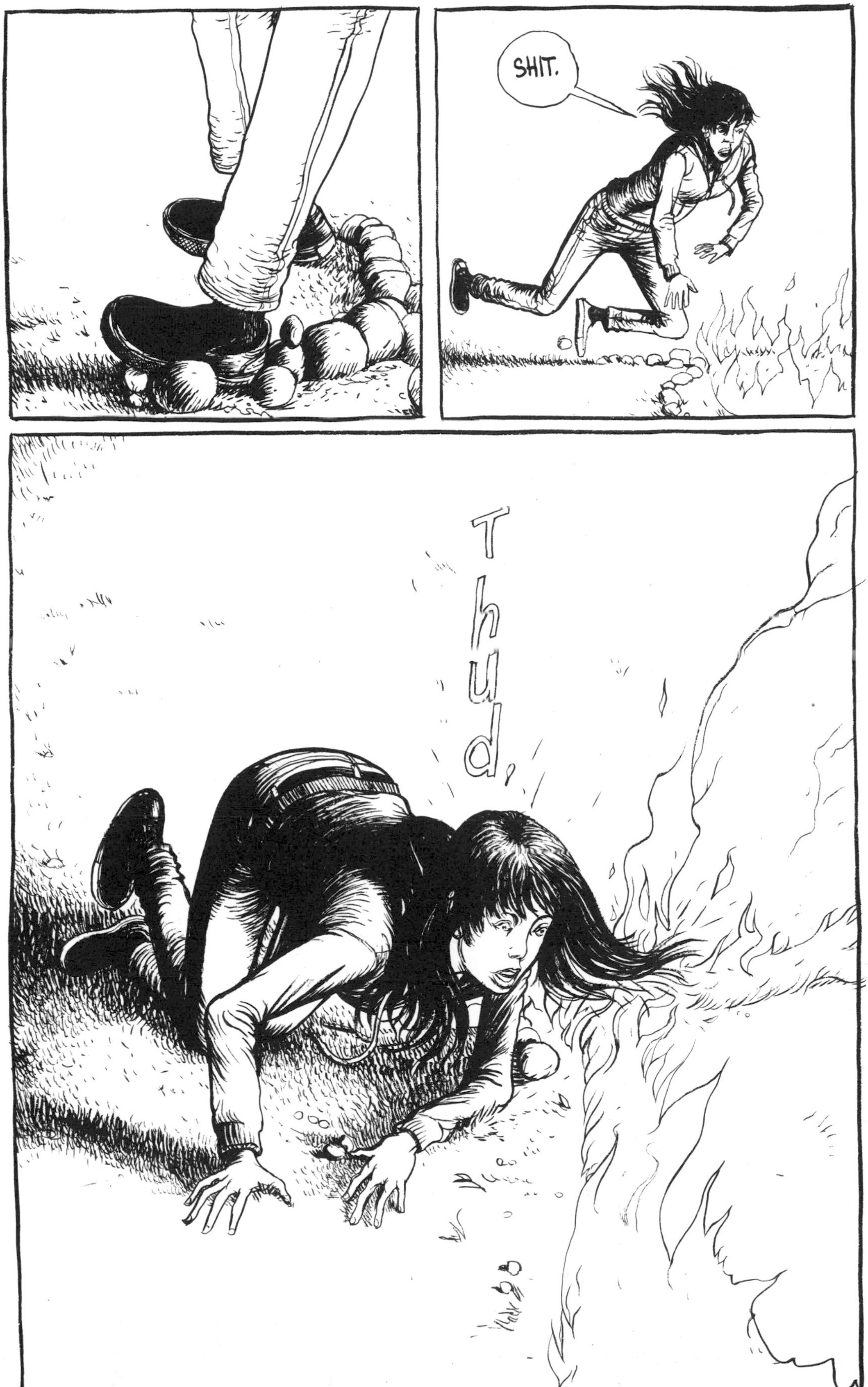
SHIT.
Thud,

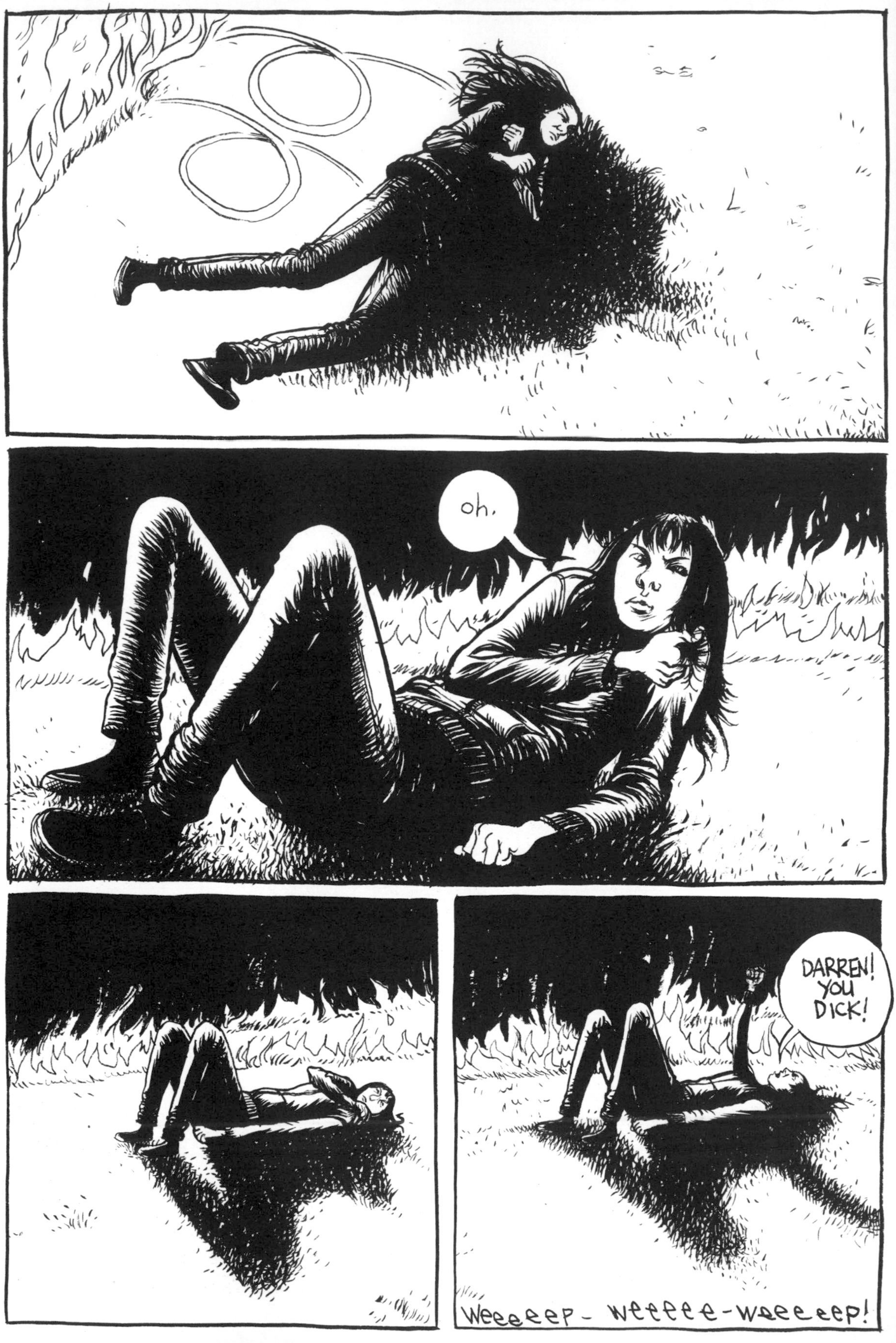
oh.
DARREN! YOU DICK!
Weeeeep- weeee-weeeeep!

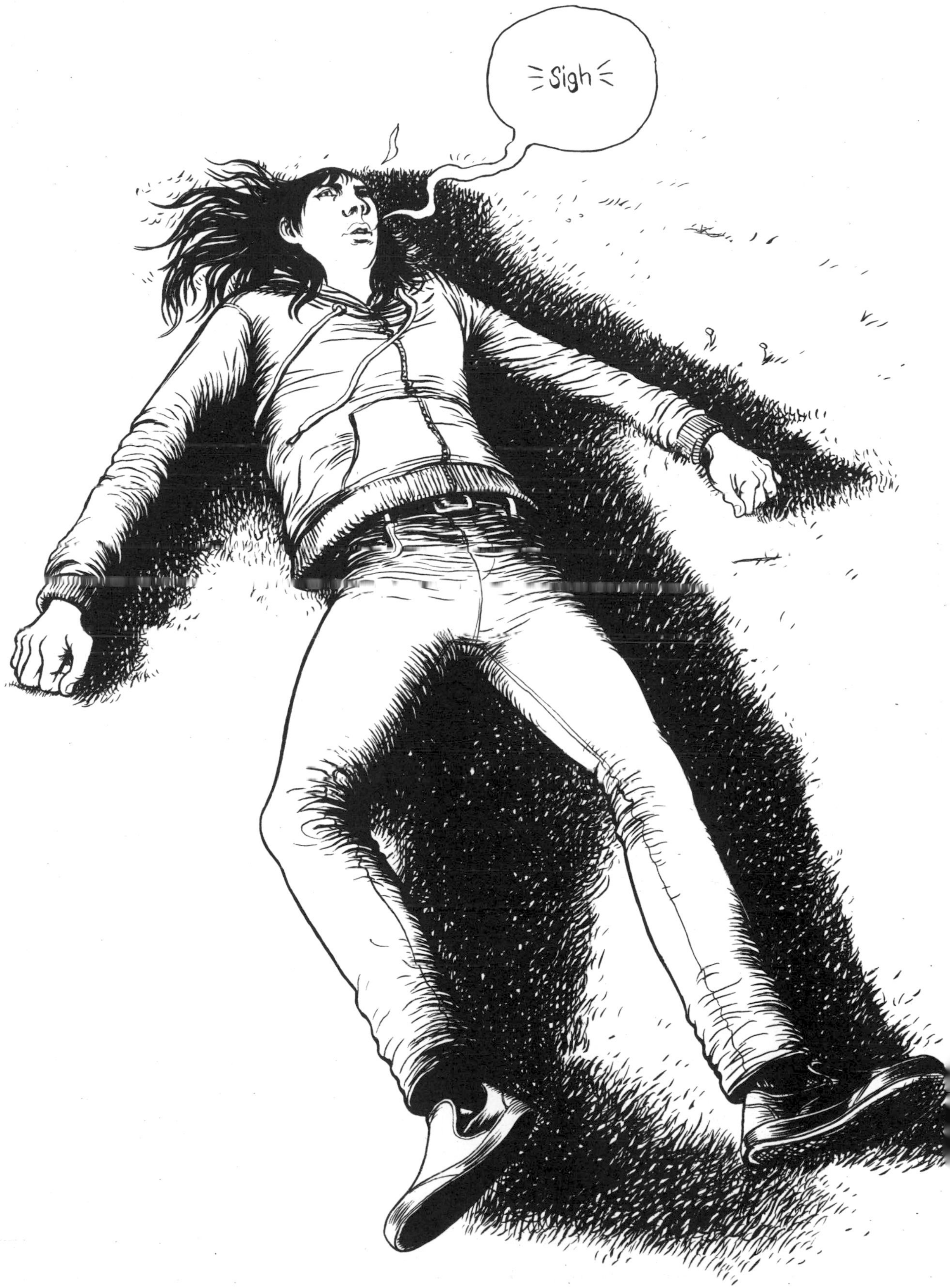
Sigh

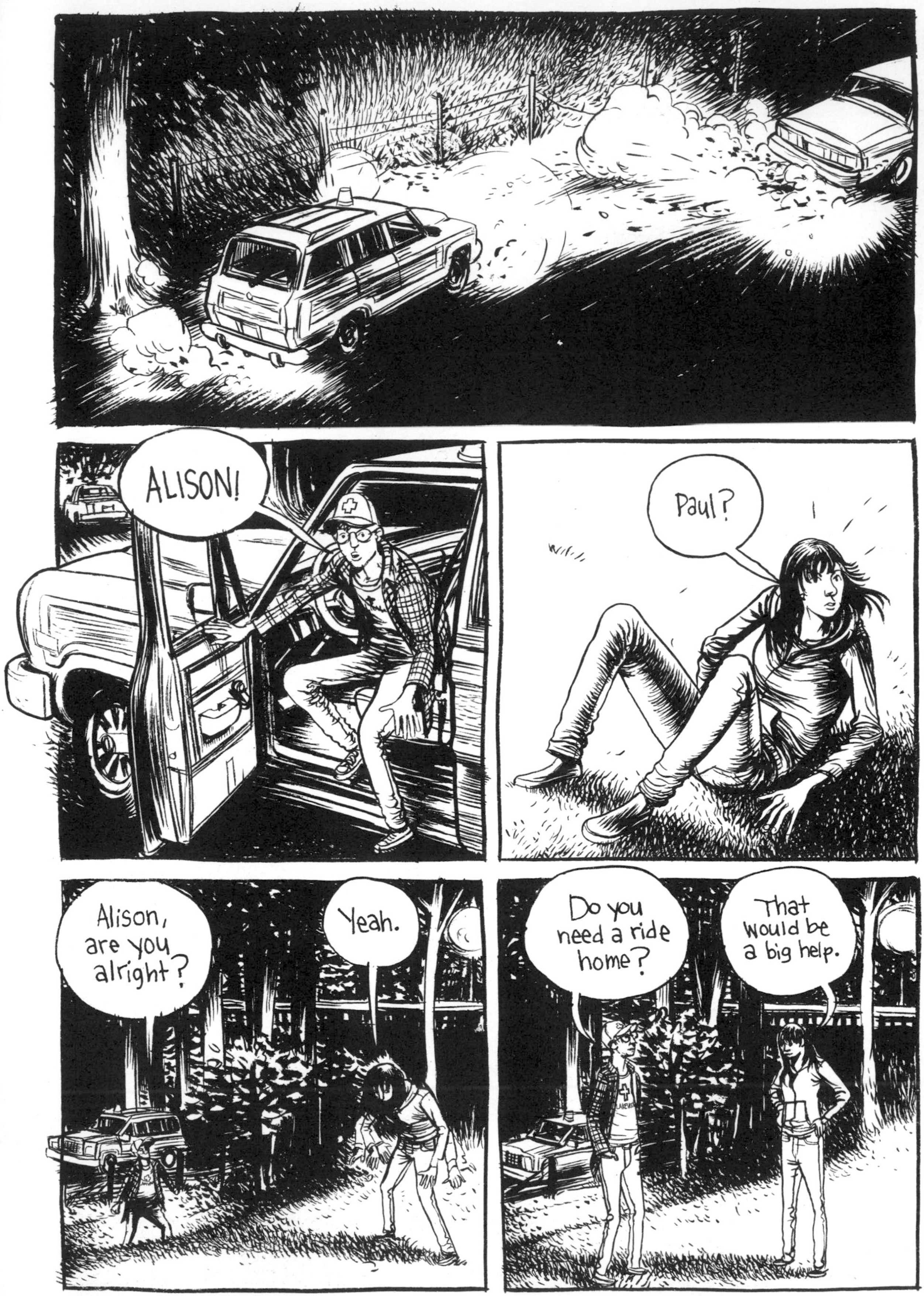
ALISON!
Paul?
Alison, are you alright?
Yeah.
Do you need a ride home?
That would be a big help.

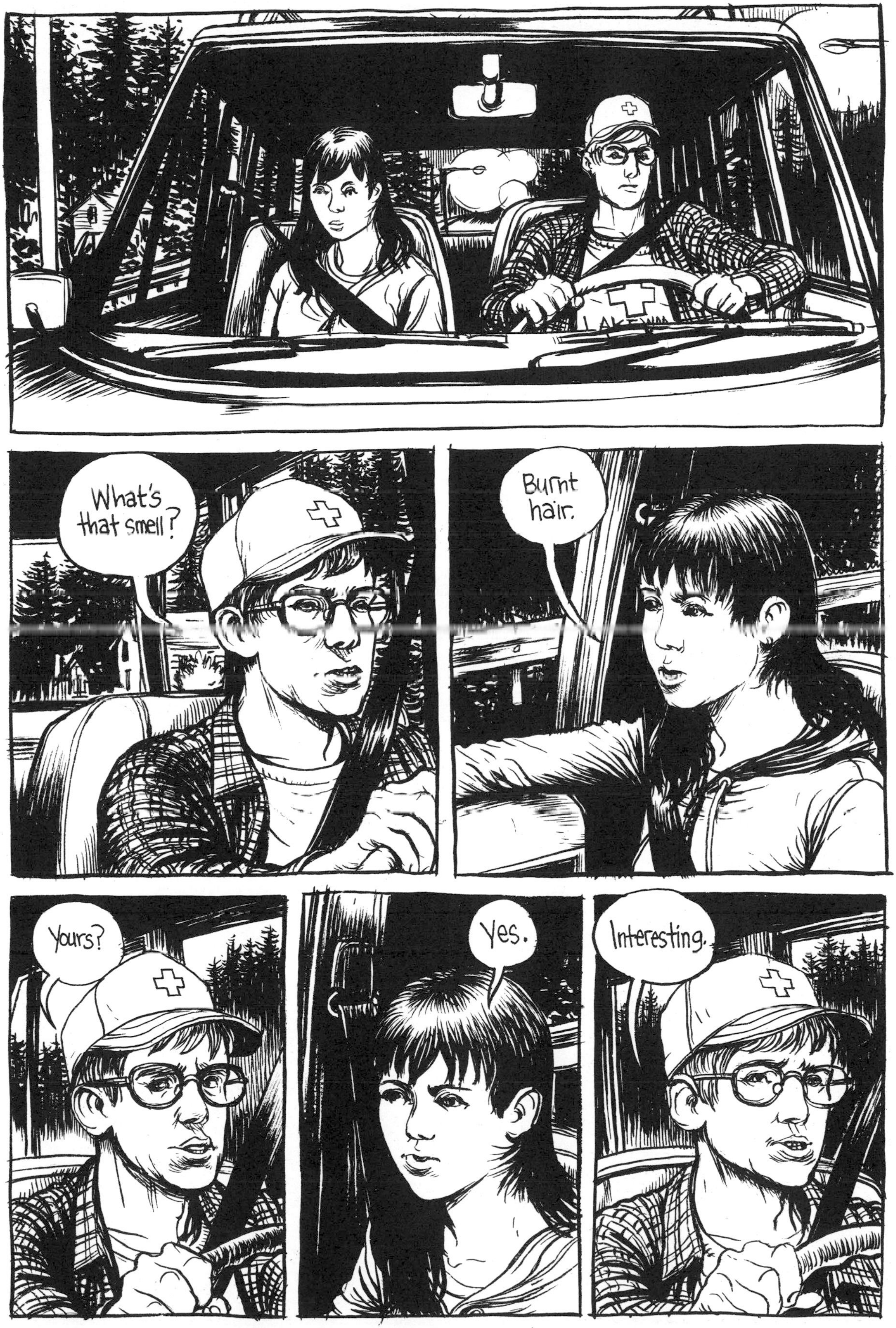

What's that smell?
Burnt hair.
Yours?
Yes.
Interesting.

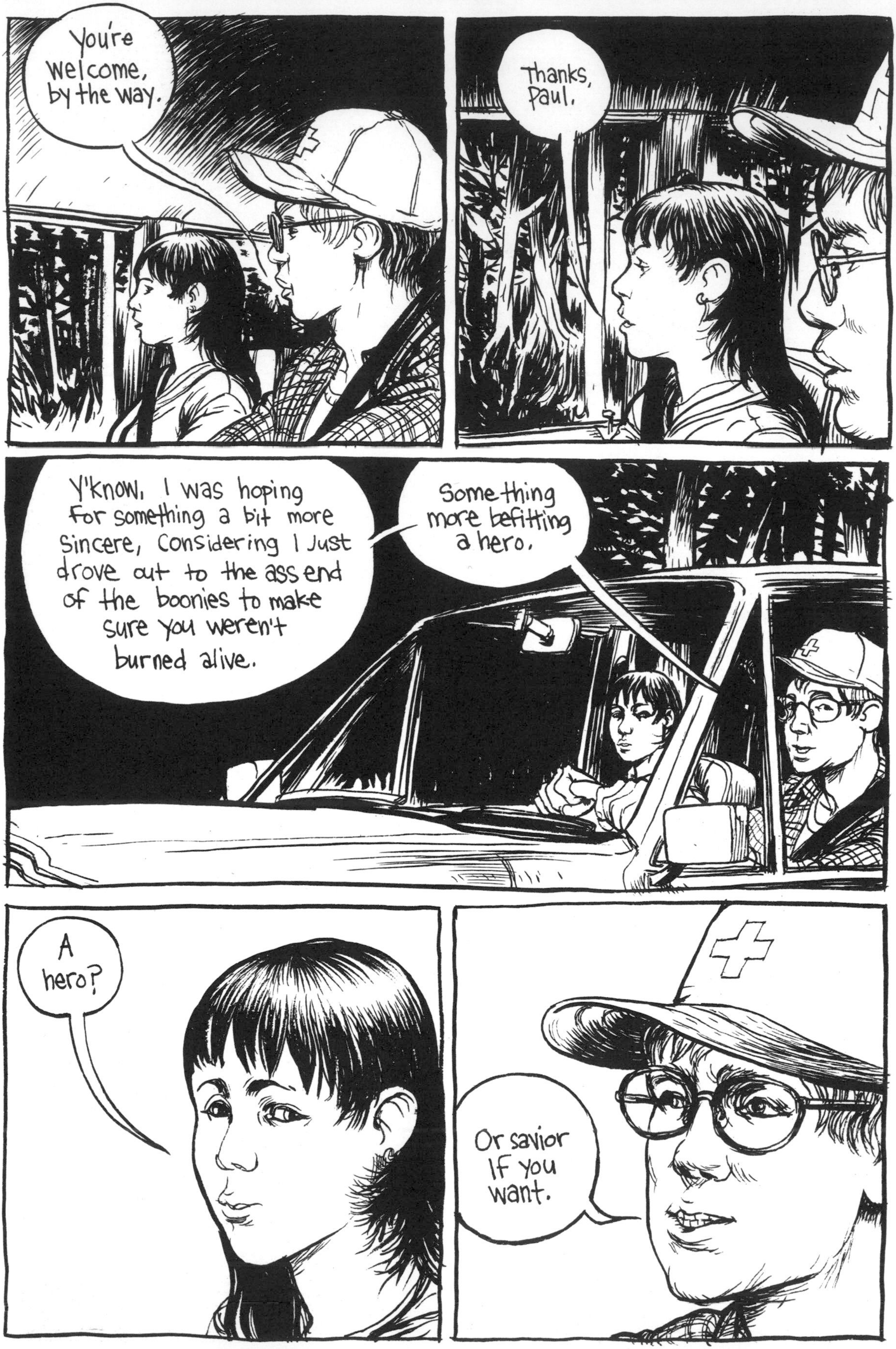
You're welcome, by the way.
Thanks, Paul.
Y'know, I was hoping for something a bit more sincere, considering I just drove out to the ass end of the boonies to make sure you weren't burned alive.
Something more befitting a hero.
A hero?
Or savior if you want.

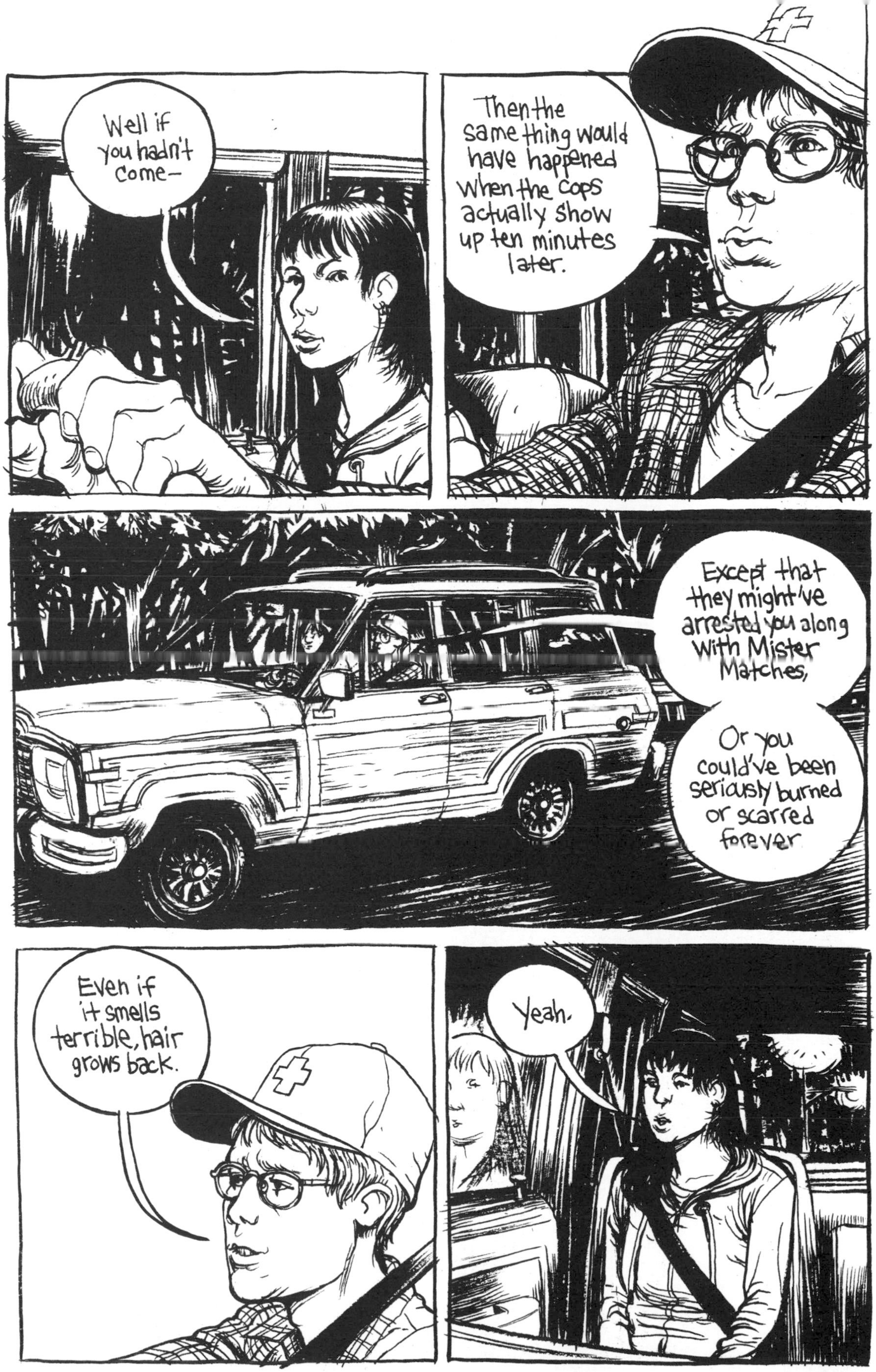

Well if you hadn't come—
Then the same thing would have happened when the cops actually show up ten minutes later.
Except that they might've arrested you along with Mister Matches,
Or you could've been seriously burned or scarred forever
Even if it smells terrible, hair grows back.
Yeah.

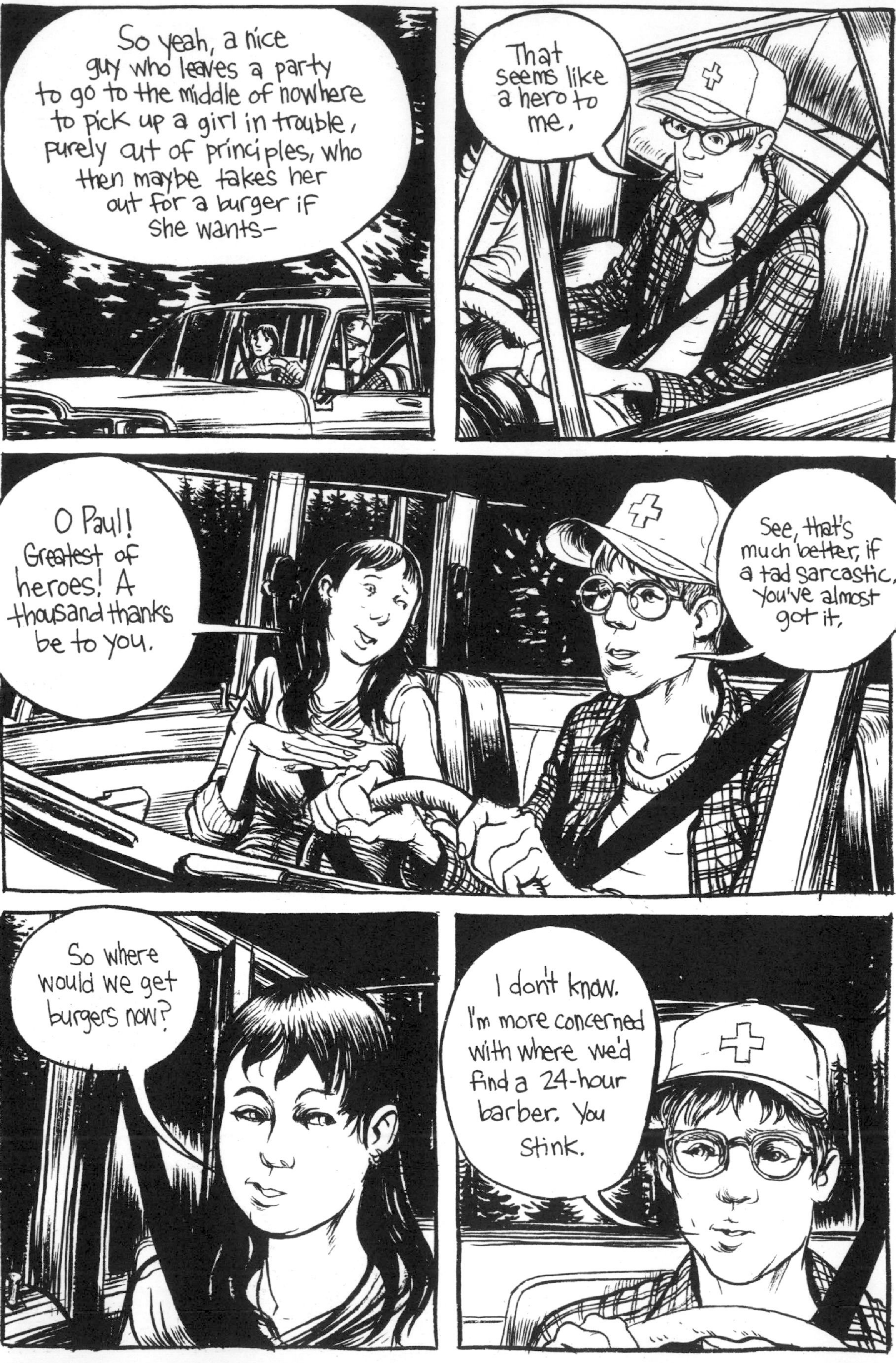
So yeah, a nice guy who leaves a party to go to the middle of nowhere to pick up a girl in trouble, purely out of principles, who then maybe takes her out for a burger if she wants-
That seems like a hero to me.
O Paul! Greatest of heroes! A thousand thanks be to you.
See, that's much better, if a tad sarcastic. You've almost got it.
So where would we get burgers now?
I don't know. I'm more concerned with where we'd find a 24-hour barber. You stink.

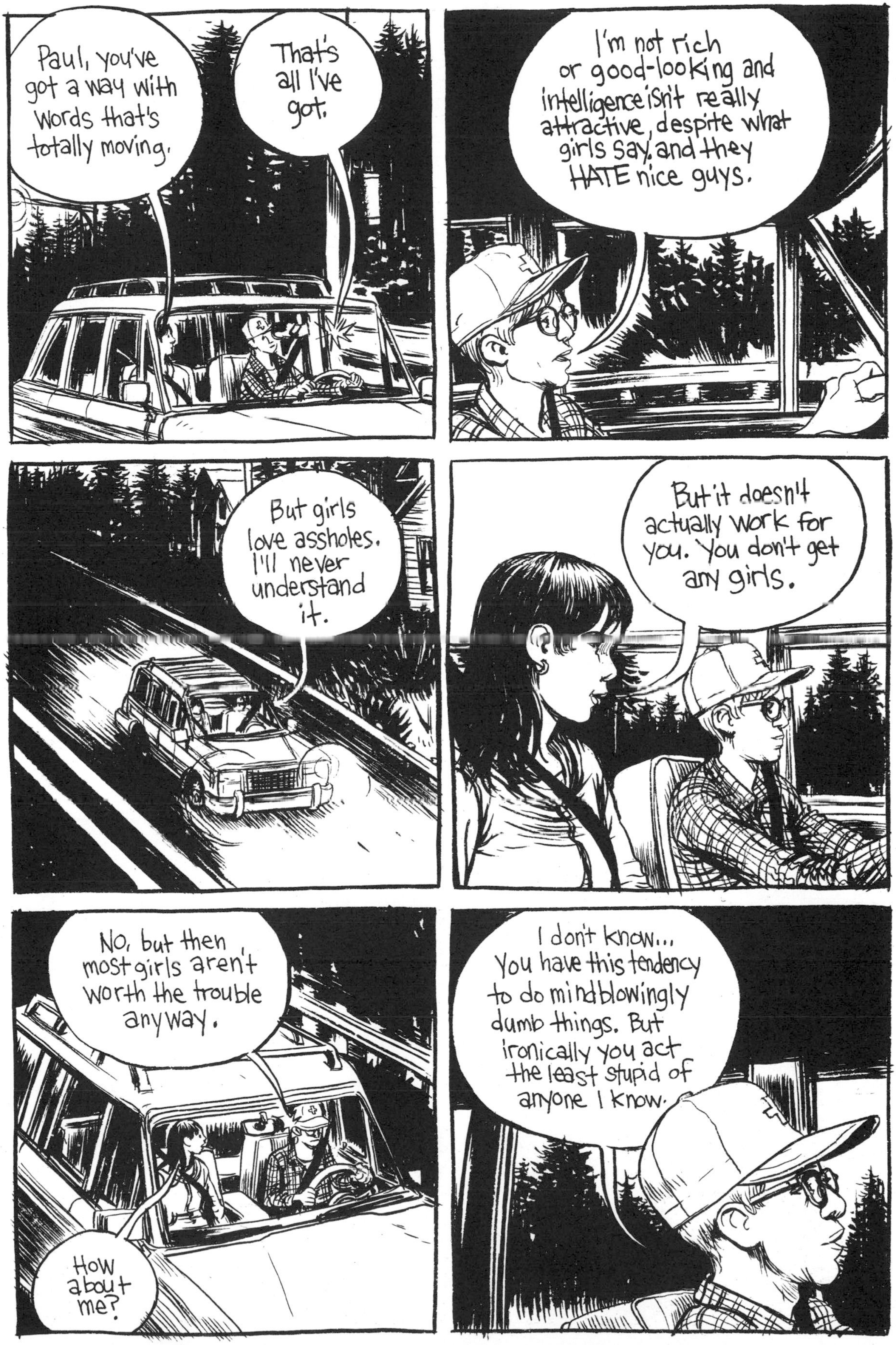
Paul, you've got a way with words that's totally moving.
That's all I've got.
I'm not rich or good-looking and intelligence isn't really attractive, despite what girls say, and they HATE nice guys.
But girls love assholes. I'll never understand it.
But it doesn't actually work for you. You don't get any girls.
No, but then most girls aren't worth the trouble anyway.
How about me?
I don't know... You have this tendency to do mindblowingly dumb things. But ironically you act the least stupid of anyone I know.

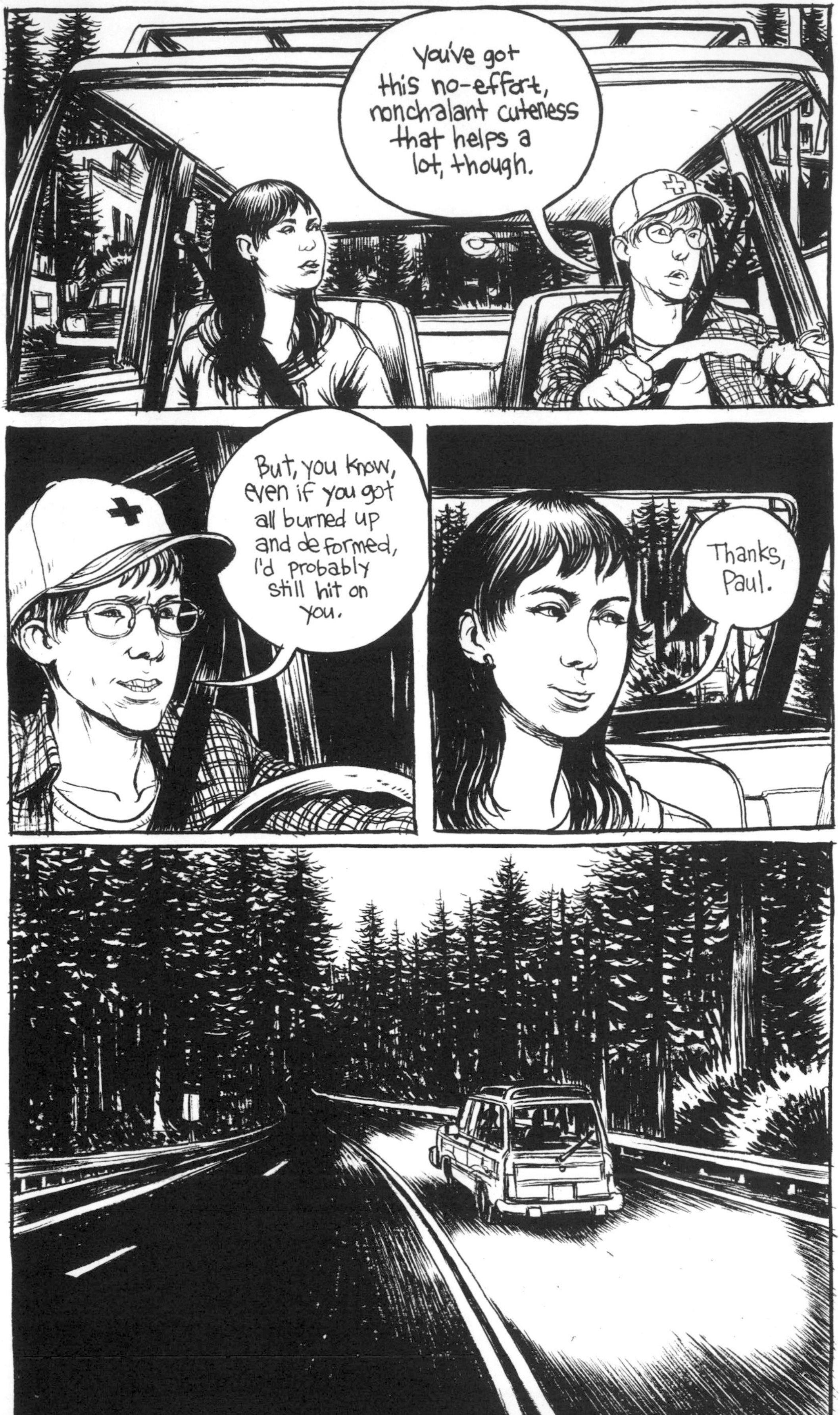
You've got this no-effort, nonchalant cuteness that helps a lot, though.
But, you know, even if you got all burned up and deformed, I'd probably still hit on you.
Thanks, Paul.

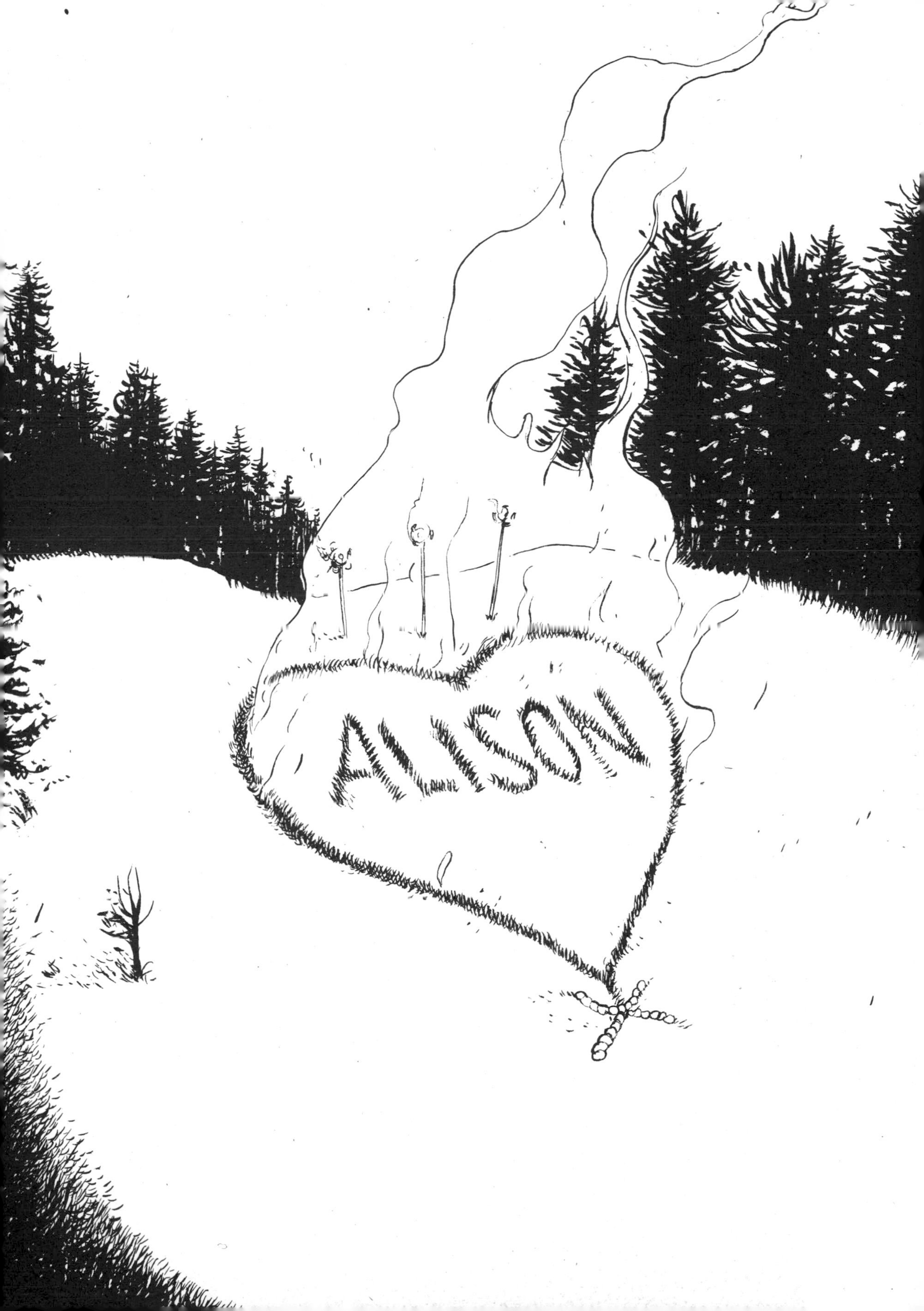
ALISON